GHETTO COPS

GHETTO COPS

On the Streets of the Most Dangerous City in America

Bruce Henderson

CONTENTS

PHOTOGRAPHY BY PHIL NELSON

COMPTON, CALIFORNIA

Incorporated in 1888, Compton was a southern California jewel during the peaceful and prosperous years after World War II. Known as "The Hub City" due to being located in the geographic center of Los Angeles County, this western-style, suburban town had neighborhood streets lined with spacious and attractive single-family homes, clean parks, good schools, a strong local tax base, and a population that was nearly 95 percent white.

A decade later, after court decisions struck down discrimination in housing, middle-class African-Americans began moving to Compton, located adjacent to the unincorporated area of Watts with its established black community. The area did not escape the societal upheavals of the 1960s. Following the Watts riots of 1965, Compton experienced "white flight" to other cities, taking with it not only affluent property owners but many businesses as well, thereby eroding the tax base and lowering the socioeconomic status of its residents. Soon, more than one-third of the city was on welfare, and its school children had the lowest reading scores in the state. The city's demographics tilted so swiftly that by the early 1970s, the population of 80,000 was 95 percent nonwhite.

Fertile ground for unemployment (40 percent among young people, who represented more than half of Compton residents) and unrest among rebellious young black males — the median age of a resident in 1970 was 20.6 — the city became notorious for its influx of violent street gangs such as the Bloods, the Crips and Sureños, all of which originated locally. The once tranquil community was overrun with gangs, guns and drugs.

Saddled with the highest incidence of major crimes per capita as measured by the FBI Crime Index, Compton became known as "The Most Dangerous City in America." From 1950 to 1970, major crimes in Compton increased nearly 3,500 percent. Through it all, the economically-depressed city was unable to hire new police officers or buy new patrol cars, radios or other equipment. Salaries were frozen, and department morale plummeted.

Policing Compton's mean streets was like patrolling a war zone. Yet, on a typical day, the 10-square-mile city had only four officers in one-man squad cars answering radio calls. At night, when it was even busier, the coverage would increase only one or two cars thanks to a few volunteer reserve officers showing up after working their day jobs.

In the summer of 1974, a young California newspaper reporter, Bruce Henderson, who was destined to become a #1 New York Times bestselling author, embedded with the Compton Police Department to observe firsthand the job of fighting such a tidal wave of street crime; as he did, he documented the daily pressures on the undermanned police force and assessed the job being done by the officers and their new chief of police, Thomas Cochée, the first black police chief in the nation's most populace state.

BRUCE HENDERSON

1

A POLICE STORY

*"Certainly people of color should be sensitive
to the injustices in our system but at the same
time we are being ripped off by people who are
the victims of a bigger system."*

—Thomas Cochée, Chief of Police

Thomas Wentworth Cochée is on the spot. He is the first
black police chief in the history of the nation's most pop-
ulous state. That in itself would be a challenge, but to
make his job doubly difficult, Cochée is police chief of a
city with the highest per capita crime rate in the United
States.

"Compton was looking for a black police chief. I
think they wanted someone who represented a blend
of law and order and community relations awareness.
Personally, I will never be a hard-core law-and-order

man, nor will I stand for the type of law enforcement that title has come to represent in recent years. I'm trying to enforce justice in the city, while at the same time sensitizing the people of Compton to the underlining reasons for crime.

"The way I perceive the police chief's job is that he is the man in the middle. He is the mediator between the police department and the community. He's a message-carrier and coordinator. The exact opposite philosophy is that the chief should be untouchable.

"Regrettably, some of my officers think this openness on my part is an eager invitation to the citizenry for personnel complaints against them. My position is that I firmly believe the citizens must have some place to go to question policemen. I would hate to live or work in a city where the police had so accessibility and no accountability."

•   •   •

Friday, 4 P.M.

Police Chief Tom Cochée is in his office on the third floor of the police headquarters building. He is being briefed by a police captain on the city's latest homicide.

"The couple parked in front of the grocery store and the lady got out while the husband waited in the car," the captain explains. "A robbery was in progress inside the store and she was ordered down on the floor with the rest of the people. One of the robbers took her purse. The two robbers exited the store and ran for their car. The husband recognized his wife's purse and tried to get it from them. They drove off and the husband followed in his car. They drove into a dead-end street and waited for him. When he pulled alongside, they blasted him in the face with both shotgun barrels."

"Oh, Lord," Cochée says. "Did we get them?"

"No. We're working on it."

• • •

On July 1, 1973, Cochée, 41, who has an M.A. in public administration (and a B.A. in law enforcement), was appointed Police Chief of Compton, California, a predominantly black Los Angeles suburb of 78,000 people that was part of the Watts riot battleground in 1965 and was the scene of 45 homicides in 1972. With some 1400 vacant structures and a third of its citizens on welfare, the city is one of the most economically depressed in the state. The law-abiding citizens of Compton live in fear of gang warfare, which according to police is responsible for 30% of the city's homicides. The west side is the territory of a black gang called the Piru, a local Compton gang that numbers about 150. The east side is the domain of the Compton Crips, the local branch of a huge black gang that numbers between 4000 and 6000 full-fledged members countywide.

When Cochée became chief the morale of the well-integrated 138-man Compton Police Department was at an all-time low. At least part of the reason was the former white chief of police, who for the past several years was lackadaisically serving out his time in order to draw full retirement benefits.

Cochée served notice early that things would be different. A sharp administrator, he realized things couldn't be changed overnight. But he began immediately showing his personalized approach to police administration by attending briefings of the patrolmen (something the former chief hadn't done once in 20 years), responding to radio calls in his unmarked car, ordering "salt and pepper" patrol teams of white and black officers, instituting a "participatory management program" that encourages all members of the department to get involved in the decision-making process, and transferring the training bureau to the Office of the Chief of Police so that he could personally design the all-important curriculum for the officers. And, a shock to some people, he called a meeting with all the gang leaders. "They were curious about me and I wanted to know who the leaders were," Cochée says. "I gave them the word."

Implementation of these and other "progressive" policies during Cochée's first few weeks led some members of the community and the police department itself to believe they had hired a soft, liberal chief who would undoubtedly prove ineffectual in such a hard-core area. But to Cochée, being progressive doesn't mean coddling criminals. Instead, he believes a progressive law enforcement administrator is one who is flexible and can mold a program to fit the community. He has labeled his program in Compton "fair and firm" law enforcement.

On the line for Tom Cochée are all the principles and theories he has developed over the years, both in the classroom and on the street. He is aware of the racial pressure on him. Being the first black chief in the state, he will be used as either a model of success or failure, depending on what happens in the city of Compton from the first day of July on.

• • •

Friday, 5 P.M.
Chief Cochée steps into Lt. Art Taylor's office to go over tonight's battle plans. Taylor, a black, will be in charge of the gang details for tonight's football game between Compton and Dominguez high schools. As usual here, the real battle won't be on the field between the football teams but on the streets between the Piru and Crips.

Friday, 5:15 P.M.
Cochée goes into the jail. A young black prisoner is being processed for release. "Hey, Dickson, why do you keep comin' in here?" Cochée asks the youth.

"Ain't been here in a long time," prisoner Dickson says.

"You've been in here three times since I've been here. That's been not quite three months. Would a job help?"

"Yeah."

"If I get you a job will you stop drinking?"

"Yeah."

"Okay, we're going to try to come up with some more jobs. Don't blow it. What were you in for this time?"

"Busted for loitering."

"Over at Compton High? Yeah, we're gonna keep the pressure on there. Stay away."

Dickson, 17, who dropped out of high school some time ago, nods his head unconvincingly.

"Take it easy, Dickson," Cochée says, leaving.

Outside the jail, Cochée says he hopes he will be able to find some local jobs for youngsters like Dickson. But some of the gang members aren't interested in gainful employment, he admits. He says the city's mayor, Doris Davis—the first black woman in the country to be elected mayor of a moderate-sized city—recently came up with 225 temporary jobs for youth.

"When we had a public meeting at city hall and the wage of $1.65 an hour was announced, a lot of kids started giggling. Only a small portion of the jobs were taken by gang members. A few of them asked me after the meeting if I would work for $1.65 an hour. I said, 'Hell, no, I've got two college degrees.' This one kid looked at me and said, 'Shoot, man, I'll keep my gun before I'll work for $1.65 an hour!'"

Friday, 5:30 P.M.

In the communications center, Cochée asks the duty sergeant if there is a patrol car nearby that is clear. All but one of the cars are busy on calls, which is not unusual here. Cochée tells the sergeant he wants to ride with the car that is clear. The chief returns to his office and straps his Colt .38 Detective Special onto his belt, under his wide-lapelled sport coat.

Friday, 5:40 P.M.

The patrol car is waiting in the parking lot behind the police building. Behind the wheel is black Officer Dick Spicer, 27, a four-year veteran of the department and a native of Compton. (Spicer: "I decided to become a cop because I wanted to do something for Compton. This is my home. I'm not going anywhere.") Cochée sits in the front seat on the passenger side. In a few minutes they are eating a quick dinner at a local pancake house.

They are back on patrol 30 minutes later. They drive slowly down neighborhood streets and are often waved to by the residents, many of whom have bars on their windows to keep out would-be burglars. There are several deserted houses on each block. "The city has about 1,400 vacant structures," Cochée says. "Most of them are federally insured residences that have reverted to governmental ownership." The gangs vandalize them before new tenants move in. As fast as they are fixed up they are vandalized again. So they are just boarded up. And that poses a real police problem. The gangs use the deserted buildings for graffiti, writing on the walls with canned spray paint. There are few obscenities, mostly the graffiti consists of names of people and gangs. "Frostie C/C." (C/C stands for Compton Crips.) "Vamp C/C." "King Need." "Red Dog." "Still Bill C/C." "Boot Hill Crips." "Red Bone A/C." "Compton Crip Ducks." "Top Cat." "Get Debra Here." "Too Cool." Cochée says the police department is recording the locations of the defaced property, in anticipation that the city will get some federal funds for youth in the city to go around and paint over the graffiti. "I have this dream," Cochée says wistfully, "that if we keep painting over it, and provide some more recreational programs in town, the defacing will stop."

Police Chief Tom Cochée stands amidst Compton's ever-present graffiti.

Friday, 6:40 P.M.

Officer Spicer and Cochée are driving through another section of town. Here there are only $70,000 and $80,000 homes. It is a rank paradox to the rest of Compton.

"Is this Compton city?" Cochée says incredulously.

"Yes."

"Ever any trouble here?"

"No," Spicer says. "I don't think the street people know it exists."

Cochée marvels at the sprawling homes, high brick fences and manicured lawns and trees. "Some chiefs really have it easy," he finally manages. "Imagine a town like this. All there is in this kind of neighborhood is an occasional accidental swimming pool drowning, a little marijuana smoking and some wife swapping."

Spicer pulls into a narrow alley behind the expensive homes and continues his patrol. All the homes have garages in the back and high fences around their property.

"It just occurred to me," Cochée says. "If someone had it in mind, he could hide behind one of these walls with a shotgun or rifle and blast you away when you come in here."

Friday, 6:55 P.M.

The squad car is flagged down by a black man in his early forties. Cochée rolls down his window.

"I have this problem," the man says. "Some kids are shooting guns down in the park near my house. I know one of the kids, he's a good boy but he's gotten in with the wrong company. I have worked hard for my family. All my life I worked hard and obeyed the law. I have six kids. You know what I mean?"

Cochée says he knows. The man gives him a description of the car the youths are shooting from. Cochée asks if he knows where they are headed.

"I heard them say they were going to the Compton-Dominguez football game later," the man answers.

Cochée thanks him. Officer Spicer guns the car ahead. He calls on the radio for assistance. He knows the park.

"There's two ways in, Chief," Spicer says. "If we go in the front they'll be able to see us, but the back way they can't. We'll go in the back door."

Two blocks from the park Spicer pulls next to the waiting cover car. "We're going in on Chester Street," Spicer tells the other officers. "You cover the front."

Spicer races around a corner, then kills the headlights. The darkened, tree-studded park is in sight. He slowly cruises through the deserted park until he reaches the other end. The cover car, now visible at the front of the park, reports over the radio that no one has come out. They've gotten away this time.

Friday, 7:20 P.M.

Chief Cochée is back in the police headquarters parking lot, talking to his two plainclothes gang-detail men. Both of them are white. Detective Thomas Barclay is a big man, tall and with broad shoulders. He and the other officer, a reserve, are wearing short-sleeve sport shirts, which cover but do not conceal the bulky presence of their guns strapped onto their belts. Tonight their assignment is to keep tabs on the Piru gang, while another two-man gang detail will be doing the same with the Crips. The idea is to keep the gangs separated and not let them get involved in the big street fight that neither side will try to avoid.

Friday, 7:45 P.M.

The "gang car" driven by Barclay is cruising down the street in front of Compton High and Cochée is following in the unmarked car. The game has already started and the bright stadium lights illuminate the streets for several blocks.

Suddenly, the police radio crackles: "A gang of 70 walking south toward the school."

Here they come, a half a block away. The Crips are walking two abreast down the sidewalk, at a quickened pace, hurrying to get to the game. When the front of the line is even with his car, Cochée stops in the middle of the street and begins counting heads as they pass. Two, four, six. . . . The black gang members are walking in a disciplined, military fashion. Twenty-two, 24, 26. . . . Many have bowler or top hats on, and some are swinging canes from their arms. Most of them are well-dressed in the latest colorful ghetto styles. They all appear young, some very young. Cochée explains that the gangs use the youngest among them to do the shooting. ("The bigger, older leaders know that if they got caught shooting they would go to state prison. So they order the young kids out. And the kids will do anything they are told because they want to be part of the gang.") Cochée is still counting. Forty-two, 44, 46. . . . Suddenly, a strange figure looms in the middle of the gang. It's Hoss-like Barclay, looking strangely out of place with his white face and yellow sport shirt. He is marching right in the middle of the gang members, telling them to keep it cool.

"Look at that," Cochée says unbelievingly. "That's neat!"

Friday, 8:10 P.M.

Inside the high-school stadium it's quiet, for now. The gangs are sitting on different sides of the field. Cochée is talking to a middle-aged black man who is a high-school administrator.

"I want to talk to you next week about parental control on campus," Cochée tells the administrator.

"I'm ready to talk about it any time," the administrator replies.

"You've got some parents in this area who would like to help. You should utilize them."

Barclay comes down from the stands, where he's been talking with the gang leaders. "They parked their cars about six blocks away and walked in," he tells Cochée.

Cochée decides to make a move. "Let's check that address we heard might be raided. Now's a good time because they probably think they have the entire police force busy at the game."

Cochée, Barclay, and the reserve officer leave the stands. On their way out of the stadium more people are coming in to the game. Every man, woman, and child is being frisked for weapons.

Friday, 8:40 P.M.

The two unmarked police cars cruise slowly down the pitch-black residential street. "A lot of gang members live on this block and the word is the other gang is going to shoot 'em up," Cochée says. Suddenly the sound of a gunshot rings out and it's very close. Cochée pulls next to Barclay's car. "The next block over," the chief says. Both cars race down the block and screech around the corner. Barclay goes on ahead and Cochée stops, puts the car in reverse, and backs up. He has spotted a car parked in the darkened driveway of a boarded-up house. He takes a small flashlight from the glove compartment and gets out to check the car. Then, carefully, he pokes around the front of the house. Finding nothing unusual, he gets back into the car and drives to the end of the block, where Barclay and the reserve officer have gotten out of their car and are talking to a small group of teen-agers. Barclay comes over to the chief. "These guys live here," he says. "They said there was shooting in here last night. They came in two Buick Rivieras and had shotguns. This guy here dove under the car when it all started."

"Oh, damn," Cochée groans. "Damn, damn."

Friday, 9:35 P.M.

Back in the stadium, Cochée is wandering through the people-packed stands and without warning is caught in a panicking surge of humanity trying to move away from an apparent fight. When the chief and two school security guards finally get through the crowd there is a teen-age boy down. The team doctor leaves the sidelines and comes into the stands. Everyone is afraid the youth has been knifed or shot and some of his gang-member friends are getting hot. The doctor says the youngster has suffered an epileptic fit. Cochée tells the officers to pass the word to the gang. Further down more fisticuffs break out and a school guard manages an exasperated, "Oh, shit," before charging through the crowd to reach the new fight scene. As the football game nears an end the tension is building in the stands. The guards and police herd the Piru gang over to one end of the stands where they can keep a closer watch on them. The scoreboard clock shows only a few minutes left to play.

Cochée leaves the stadium to be out on the streets when the game is over. On his way into the stadium is Lt. Taylor. He asks Cochée what the situation is inside.

"Oh, all kinds of crap is going on," Cochée says. "I think it's pretty well under control now. If what I've seen is any indication, I think we'll have to worry when the game is over. We'll have to stay pretty close to them."

• • •

In 1941, when Tom Cochée was nine years old, his grandmother put him on a train in New York to join his mother and stepfather in Los Angeles.

In California, he was the only black youngster in his elementary school. "The first day the principal called me into his office and said he had had two 'colored' in his school before and never had any trouble from them, so he wasn't expecting any from me."

Cochée, an only child, dropped out of school at age 16 and married his childhood sweetheart, Pat. At the time he had a promising athletic career as a middle distance runner, with the Olympics his goal. But being married and with a young family on the way (eventually four children), Cochée soon found these were the more necessary things in life. He took two jobs, collecting eggs at a nearby egg farm and mopping floors for a janitorial service. By the time he was 21 he had been hired and fired from several jobs, so he started his own maintenance business, mopping and waxing office floors after business hours.

"I wasn't happy," Cochée remembers. "I had this thing about being a Negro janitor. It bothers me to this day."

When Cochée went to the Pasadena courthouse one day to pay a traffic fine he saw the young, uniformed police officers looking proud and gallant, and on the way out—before he reached the bottom step—he decided to go back to school and try to become a policeman. He got his high-school diploma, then took some college classes while taking every available police officers' examination in the area. When he was hired by the Los Angeles County Sheriff Department in the early fifties there was an unwritten quota on the number of blacks allowed into the department. "I thought I'd be a deputy forever," he recalls. "There wasn't even a black corporal in the department."

But Cochée eventually made sergeant, the youngest black at the time to do so. During the 1965 Watts riot (which actually spilled over into Compton), Cochée worked the "community relations" detail on the streets of Watts and Compton. "I was on the street in short sleeves and without a gun, doing intelligence work," he explains. "My reactions were amazement, frustration, and anger. It seemed to me that better police techniques were needed. I saw policemen standing around not enforcing the law. It was a completely open town." As to whether he thinks such a riot potential exists in Compton today, Cochée says, "The potential exists, but I don't think the black psyche is in that condition. Such acts are senseless, utter frustration."

In the same year (1965) Cochée quit the sheriff's department. ("There were no black lieutenants on the force and I was ambitious.") He went to work as an investigator for the Los Angeles County Public Defender's Office. After taking college classes off and on for 16 years, Cochée finally received his B.A. degree in police science and nine months later his M.A. in public administration. The next four years he was coordinator of the Administration of Justice Department at Merritt College, Oakland, California.

• • •

Friday, 9:55 P.M.
The two gangs have exited the stadium from opposite sides of the field. Sitting in his car a block away from the stadium, Cochée watches as the Piru march

by. Barclay is again walking with them. Cochée follows slowly in his car. Over the radio comes a report that the Crips are walking in a direction that will allow the two gangs to converge. It's like a big chess game, and somebody has apparently made the wrong move. The Piru are now strung out for two blocks.

"The fight's on!" the police radio announces. "Clubs . . . sticks!"

Cochée, who has taken off his coat, bounds out of the car and runs down the block toward the Piru. He finds Barclay, who tells him someone pushed the panic button. It was a false alarm; there's no fight. But the Piru, now 80 to 100 strong, are ready for the Crips if they should meet on the street.

"Hey, this is sumpthin," one gang member regales. "We got po-leese protection!"

"Not for long," Barclay promises. "You keep this shit up and you'll all be in jail."

Cochée goes back and gets his car and rejoins the procession, cruising slowly behind. The gang mysteriously divides in the darkness, and suddenly Barclay and the other officer are not in sight. Cochée alone is following a group of 50 gang members. They continue for several dark blocks, without another policeman or police car in sight. Cochée marvels at the discipline the gang members are showing. "That one little guy in the bowler hat, Herman, is in charge. He's got a lot of control over them. He's on our side now, trying to avoid a fight, but I don't know what his motivation is."

The gang members stop at the end of a particularly dark residential street. Cochée pulls his car over to the curb and gets out. Some of the members are getting into their cars, parked here for the march in to the game. Others are just standing around. Cochée walks up to a small group and recognizes one youth as the guy who started a fight in the stands. "I don't want you coming to a game like that again," Cochée tells him firmly.

"I wasn't high," he says.

"You were drunk. Don't do it again. I want you guys to go home now."

Cochée walks down the sidewalk telling the gang members it is past curfew. More of them begin getting into cars. Others are walking away in different directions, in groups of two and three. ("To have busted them all for curfew violation now would have been harassment.")

As Cochée goes back to his car a woman resident standing on her porch calls out to him, "Hey, Chief, don't leave till it's over."

"We'll be in the area," he tells her.

Cochée gets on the radio and finds out the Crips have broken up. The gang threat is over for the night; the young thrill-seekers have been thwarted by close police surveillance.

"Crime is a young man's game," he explains. "The greatest rate of crimes is committed by males between the ages of 16 and 26 years. Half the residents of this city are under the age of 19."

He thinks many of the young gang members who take up so much of the police department's time are scarred by self-hatred. "This comes from the lack of respect that exists in the homes they come from. The parents have no respect for themselves or the children, so it would be foolish to expect the children to have any respect for themselves or anyone else.

"Children are born and they are allowed to grow and that is the extent of parental responsibility. The cause of crime here is unwanted and unloved children."

Saturday, 8:15 A.M.

At a special meeting of the all-black city council—attended by a few interested spectators, the press, and Cochée—the black city manager is allowed to resign, under pressure. It is typical of the city's unstable political environment caused by its massive and so far unsolved problems. After watching the man who hired him kicked out of his own job, Cochée is philosophical.

"When I go somewhere else, whether I'm fired from this job or quit, I expect another city manager to say, 'Well, Cochée, I know what you were up against in Compton. That's a helluva job. I think with your credentials you can do the job here.'" Cochée is silent for a moment, then adds, "With what the situation is here, I can't really go down, only up. It's an excellent opportunity to prove what I can do."

Saturday, 9 A.M.

Cochée enters the squad room, where the oncoming patrolmen are being briefed by the duty sergeant, and sits in the back of the room. A sign on the wall reads: ACT—DON'T REACT, PRACTICE SELF-CONTROL. There are 11 officers present, three whites and eight blacks. The overall departmental ratio is 50% white, 40% black, and 10% Chicano, while eight out of 10 Compton residents are black. (Cochée: "Even though most ghetto riots have been started by white officers making an arrest, all-black officers are not the answer here. Blacks can be insensitive, too. Training and attitude is the answer.")

The sergeant says, "A block party today on your beat, Smith. Could be a trouble spot. A lot of assholes live there. . . . A shooting yesterday. Blew up two guys. Shot one in the body and the other in the groin. Both are in the hospital in bad shape. . . . On the teletype LAPD has a warrant on two subjects. There aren't any indications they're going to be in our area but I'll give them to you anyway. Three male Negroes, black over brown. Suspects are armed and dangerous. They previously attempted to use hand grenades on arresting officers."

The officers move uneasily in their chairs and from the back of the room Cochée says softly, "Damn."

". . . They're with the Republic of New America. The Afro-American Liberation Army may attempt to link up with them," the sergeant adds.

After several seconds of silence, the sergeant offers, "If you see three guys with bulges in their pockets, be careful."

"Yeah, get out of there," a patrolman agrees.

When the sergeant is finished with the briefing, Cochée walks to the front of the room. "Good morning, officers," he says smiling.

"Good morning, Chief," they say in unison.

"I'd like to say a few words to you this morning," Cochée says. "I don't know if you've ever been asked what the goal is of our police department but someone asked me that a week or so ago. This organization exists to reduce crime and do some public relations when we get the chance. Fair and firm is still the word.

"I'm glad to see some of you guys are interested in getting more education. If anyone knows of a course he wants to take, let us know so we can get you registered. I was 16 years getting a B.A. If you want it, go after it. Those of you who don't have yours, keep working for it.

"Okay, go catch me a burglar running down the street with the loot in hand. And be careful of nuts like the hand-grenade crew!"

Later, Cochée admits he's not anxious to put women officers on patrol (the department has two women officers in the detective bureau). "But I won't resist it," he says. "If there's ever an argument against it, Compton is it. I've heard though that they have worked out in Washington, D.C. If women can control the streets in D.C. they can control Compton."

Cochée thinks women officers would be advantageous on calls involving family fights, rapes, child abuse, and sex crimes.

• • •

It turns into a seven-day work week for Cochée as he accepts an invitation from the Compton Jaycees to give a Sunday morning talk about the crime problem at their breakfast meeting.

In introducing Cochée, the Jaycees' young president says, "In Chief Cochée's short tenure here we have already seen a reduction in crimes. We may be Number One now but by 1974 we're going to be looking a whole lot better!" The chief is welcomed by loud applause.

"I hope the crime rate is going down," Cochée says. "But I'm too close to the trees to see the forest. All I know for sure is that we have too much crime and we are not going to put up with it. I'm tired of the Friday night 'football games' between the Crips and Piru. I know there are people in the community who are equally fed up and want to do something. But you ask yourself, what can you do?

"Well, in the last three weeks we have reactivated our police explorers' program and we need volunteer help. Or maybe you businessmen would want to think about sponsoring a local track meet for the kids. And the Compton Champs, a local boxing club, is looking for a home. I really want to see them get going. I'm telling the gang members it's not proving their manliness to drive down the street in the middle of the night shooting guns. I tell them to get into the ring if they want to prove something. Also, we need parents to help patrol our campuses. And we're always looking for more police officers to help beef up our patrols. Neighborhoods have to get closer together. The new urban neighborhood, with people not getting involved with each other, is a tool to the burglar. Become suspicious. Report it when a car has driven down your street six times in the last five minutes. Give us the make of the car so we can do something. . . . Certainly people of color should be sensitive to the injustices in our system but at the same time we are being ripped off by people who are victims of a bigger system. Crime is taking place in Compton, regrettably, so we have to join hands to form a unified front.

"We've got cats running up and down our streets shaking people down. We have to get the worst off the street, then try to deal with the others. We need the local businessmen to give us more jobs for youths and try to get them involved in the community in a positive way. To the kids who are carrying guns—I've told them if they fire their guns there's no guarantee that the police will not fire back with shotguns. If they arm themselves, then they have to accept what might happen. . . .

"Compton, Beverly Hills, Glendale, these are all fake and artificial communities that were improperly developed socially and their people have a hard time functioning healthily in the real world. But there are positive things in Compton. I see the people of the community as the strongest asset. The solution to the crime problem is human resources and involvement."

The Jaycees, a young group composed mainly of local black businessmen, have interrupted Cochée a dozen times with loud applause. When he is through, several men walk up to Cochée to shake his hand and offer their time and assistance to help solve the city's crime problem. Cochée knows the talk went over well and he is obviously pleased.

"When I came here I figured that Compton was one of the ten most difficult police chief's jobs in the nation," he explains. "I still believe that to be the case."

2

"SHOOT'EM, TOM!"

"The real reason for us carrying guns while off-duty in this city is to protect our asses."

—Officer Robert Page, Gang Detail, Compton P.D.

I just got back late last night from a four-day trip to Compton. As look through my notebook in which I intended to keep a diary of my immediate observations, I see that it is filled with readable but slightly nonsensical words that are supposed to ignite instant recall of a spellbinding or important event. For instance, these words written in large scrawl fill one page."Next call: silent alarm—no siren or red lights—gas station —car w2 occupants parked next to the rest rooms—cops approach car—very hairy—broken lock . . . bag of money. . . ."

The words do bring back the incident quite clearly, and I can even begin to feel some of the tension and

adrenaline I felt as I watched the cops-and-robbers confrontation from the backseat of the black-and-white
patrol car that night, wondering what I would do if the
cops were gunned down in front of me. Should I go for
the shotgun sitting menacingly in the dashboard bracket
and try to shoot my way out? Let's see, how the hell did
the cop say that thing is cocked? Or should I hide behind
the seat, and instantly make myself invisible? Maybe I
should grab the radio and call out: "Officer needs help!"
An utterance is sure to bring every cop within 50 miles.
Or should I just ignore the inevitable bullets? How about
running like hell?

My notebook is definitely not a diary, but I do have
notes typical of the kind I take for newspaper and magazine articles: heavy on dialogue, a few words that at the
time seemed to best describe a particular situation and
a sprinkling of names and statistics. It seems unbelievable to me now that from this scrawl in my notebook will
come prose. If I took this notebook now and locked it
in an old suitcase, what would it mean to anyone in 10
years? Hell, I'm not even sure what it will mean to me
next month. So I have to write now, tell the story while
it's still fresh in my mind and when I can still see the faces
of the people involved and still feel all the raw emotions.

Important things are happening in Compton, as
well as exciting things, sad things, shitty things. . . . It all
means something, too, but I admit I don't know what. I
just haven't come to grips with that yet. All I know for
sure is that people are killing each other. Their economic and social depression has turned inward in the worst
form of self-hate. Young manhood and womanhood is
being wasted, tragically, hopelessly; young people who

someday might have affected a worthwhile change in the system are dying, taking to their deaths an ugly, eternal pain. The victims of the high ghetto crime rate in Compton are not the well-to-do white residents of Beverly Hills and Glendale; the victims are the ghetto residents themselves. Brother killing brother. Husband killing wife. Lover killing lover. Neighbor killing neighbor. Friend killing friend. A flagrant black bloodbath.

> "And the poor have the sufferings to
> which they are fairly accustomed,
> And each in the cell of himself is
> almost convinced of his freedom."
>
> —W. H. Auden

I arrived in Compton on the afternoon of Friday, March 29, 1974, and went directly to police headquarters. Tom Cochée was waiting for me in his second-floor office, and he greeted me with a friendly smile and firm handshake.

"Everything is go here," Cochée said. "You know you have my full cooperation. And I took your last letter to a meeting of the department's supervisory personnel, and overall it looks pretty good there, too. One officer said he didn't like the word 'ghetto' used in the title, and he came up to my office later and we continued the discussion. I told him what my definition of ghetto was, and we talked about it for a while. That was the only problem, otherwise there shouldn't be any resistance."

Cochée and I went to lunch, along with the Chief's

new right-hand man, Lt. Ed Carrington, a black officer whom Cochée had just assigned to his office to be a special assistant. Cochée, a deliberate and careful man, had waited almost a year before naming an assistant. He wanted to be sure he found the right man; someone who would be supportive of him, well qualified for the administrative duties and respected by the majority of the department as well as the citizenry.

Midway through lunch, Cochée laid the bombshell on me. "I just turned down the chief's job with the City of Berkeley," he said casually. "It was $6,000 a year more and a much bigger department, but I said I wasn't interested."

"Why?" I said incredulously, my mind slightly boggled by the choice of Compton over Berkeley.

"It was just too soon," he explained carefully. "I haven't even been here a year; I've just started my program here, and to leave now would look bad. Like I'm trying to escape."

I could see the implication. First black police chief in the state of California flees from black community because he can't hack it. No, Tom Cochée has got to tough it out in Compton for a few years, and do something remarkable: like reduce the crime rate. And he knows it.

• • •

Officer Robert Page is a tall black man with a powerful, youthful physique, who bears a striking resemblance to the San Francisco 49ers' handsome flanker, Gene Washington. He is the only officer in the department who carried the title of "gang detail." Working directly under the Chief, Page is responsible for maintaining contact with the city's rival gangs; knowing ahead of time what they are planning to do, whom they are planning to shoot, who the new leaders are, who might be willing to fink, etc. Page is also the best pistol shot in the department, a definite asset when driving an unmarked detective car into a gang neighborhood, alone, to powwow with the baddies.

On the pistol range this Friday afternoon, getting in his required monthly qualifying score, Page missed very few shots. A perfect score is 300 (you get 30 shots, with a bull's eye counting 10 points, a near-miss 9, etc.). Page's score today was 292. His right arm, injured in a skiing accident and subsequently reinjured in an arrest hassle, was in a sling. He took it out of the sling to do the shooting. His best ever score is a nifty 298.

After he finished shooting the .357 magnum revolver at the black silhouette target, Page pulled in the poor paper dummy and counted the bullet holes, most of them in the distinct region of the heart.

"Shooting at a practice target is completely different than combat shooting," Page explained. "I remember a few years ago some people were upset about cops using black silhouettes for targets because supposedly we were learning to kill blacks by using black targets. I never pay much attention to that kind of shit."

Page has never shot anyone, although he had a fine opportunity to do just that not long ago. "I went to talk to a gang member at his house, and when I walked in some guy ran out the back door, carrying a shotgun. I ran through the house and out the back door after him. When I stepped out-aide both barrels were aimed at me, and I ducked just as he shot. The pelts zinged over my head. I pulled out my gun and aimed at his heart. I could have killed him right then and there, but I didn't. I don't know why. I just arrested him."

Like many cities, Compton requires its policemen to wear their guns while off duty. The universal argument is that policemen are policemen 24 hours a day and no matter where they are or with whom they are, they should be able to take decisive police action if they are witness to a crime.

"But the real reason for us carrying guns while off duty in this city is to protect our asses," Page said bluntly. "Shit, you could be out mowing your lawn and some gang guy who you've given a bad time might consider it an excellent opportunity to blow you up."

Page's off-duty weapon is a $200 silver-plated Walther with good stopping power. (Stopping power: one shot anywhere in the body will blow away enough meat to stop a guy cold in his tracks.) James Bond fans will remember the Walther. 007 used to carry a pretty Beretta until Ian Fleming's able ordinance man made him switch to a Walther before a particularly deadly mission. Reason: more stopping power. "It's the Cadillac of automatics," Page said simply, with a hint of pride. (Like most cops, Page carries a .357 while on duty.)

After target practice it's time for a cruise around town in an unmarked car. There are a few people whom Page wants to see and he invites me along to observe. Unlike some of the other officers I later ride with, Page is immediately open and cooperative; perhaps because he works directly out of the Chief's Office and is accustomed to attention and public relations. (As I learned later, the patrolmen, or "troopies" as they refer to themselves, are an altogether different breed.)

We climbed into the unmarked, light blue, four-door cop car that is supposed to look like a noncop car but fails miserably even to the eye of an untrained observer. (For all the people it fools, the word "Pigmobile" might as well be written on the door.) I'm busily talking to him about my observations of Compton—I always hog the first part of an in-depth interview so that the other person will feel more at ease and also so he'll know where I'm coming from—and it takes me a couple of minutes before I realize that Page is speeding to some unknown destination (unknown to me). A "shots fired" call had come over the radio while I was busily rapping with myself. Typically, the constant chatter of codes and voices on the police radio meant nothing to me. Like any other cop, Page had trained himself to perk up at the sound of certain codes that designate crimes. I realized two things: I would have to learn those bleeping codes and also pay more attention to the blabbering radio.

The call is to find an armed teen-ager dressed in a leather jacket in the vicinity of Park Village, an isolated rundown community of dilapidated tenements on the west side of town with a vacancy rate of nearly 90%. The village is a haven for gang activities and affords many hideouts and gun caches among the boarded-up vacant units. There are several patrol cars in the area and Page pulls up over a curb and drives out into a weeded field to cover one possible escape route from the teen-ager's last reported position. Sitting in the middle of a field, we suddenly see a shadowy figure running between two wrecked structures, heading toward us. Two uniformed cops are in pursuit, about 50 feet behind the figure. Page jumps out of the car and yells to me: "Stay put!" I offer no argument. I'm a firm believer in first-person involvement in stories, New Journalism and all that crap, but goddamn, there's a limit. I make sure I am in a good position to duck down under the dashboard. Page is now out in the open, holding his heavy .357 down at his side. I have a sinking feeling in my stomach when I remember how good of a shot he is; then the sick feeling turns to one of security. After all, some son of a bitch is coming at us with a gun. Jesus, Bob Page, don't get killed in the middle of a field by some punk wielding a Saturday Night Special!

Chief Cochée is on the scene shortly after the youth is apprehended. No shots were fired and when the kid is arrested he is unarmed. The cops are sure he dumped the gun somewhere in the tall weeds. A dozen cops search through the greenery while the young man stands sedately against a building, his hands handcuffed behind his back. Page goes over and talks to him; the other cops obviously hoping that Page, who has so many gang contacts, might get something out of the kid. But it's no good. The kid knows nothing about a gun or a shooting or fleeing from cops. He was just taking a stroll when all these pigs came out of the bushes at him.

Cochée looks curiously at the youngster. "Isn't that a shame. Here he is out jogging on a peaceful afternoon and the cops come down on him like this. I tell you, law-abiding citizens just don't have a chance anymore."

Cochée kicks through the weeds, too, for a few minutes. "We'd almost have to step on the thing to find it here," he says. "We'll have to put a metal detector on our next year's budget."

• • •

When Tom Cochée was offered the Compton job, his wife, Pat, was vehemently opposed to it. "Look, Tom, I spent a good deal of my life trying to get out of the ghetto," she argued, "and I am not going back!" She had since relented.

I asked Cochée how he managed to change her mind. He said: "I moved out!" Pat got one concession, though. Their junior high school-age daughter was still attending public school in a not-so-nearby beach community. But Pat, who drove her to and from school each day, felt it was well worth the long drive to keep the girl out of Compton's "armed-camp schools."

The Cocheés were now managing a large apartment complex, rent free. It was good for the doctor-owner because word was getting around town that the Chief of Police lived there, and potential burglars would presumably think twice before hitting the place.

But obviously the word hadn't gotten out to everyone. One day in the middle of the afternoon, Tom and Pat were returning home from the store in the Chief's unmarked car, and as he turned into the alley behind the apartment, he noticed someone straighten up suddenly from behind a parked car. The car happened to be his son Tommy's, a University of Southern California triple jumper, who lived with them. As the young man darted away from the car and headed for the other end of the alley, Cochée reached in his glove compartment and took out his revolver. By this time the volatile Pat was yelling: "Get him! Get that son of a bitch!" Tom sped the car down the alley, and as he passed his son's car he saw a long siphoning hose running from the car's gas tank to a large gasoline can. (It must be remembered that this was during the so-called oil shortage and the days of two-hour-long lines at service stations. Gasoline was a valuable commodity.) Cochée's car reached the man just as he was climbing into a car parked at the other end of the alley. Cochée blocked the car with his, then jumped out, holding the pistol in the traditional two-handed policeman's grip and pointing it at the man. "Freeze! Police!" On Cochée's command, the gas siphoner and his accomplice got out of the car very slowly and carefully, with their hands reaching for the sky.

By this time Pat had jumped out of the unmarked car and had come around to stand next to Tom. "Shoot 'em, Tom!" she beseeched. "Kill the bastards! Where's the nearest tree, I wanna hang these niggers!" (Yes, Pat is black, too. But that's the way she talks about blacks she considers to be bad news.)

"Those poor guys didn't know what to make of it," Tom laughed later. "Pat was screaming for me to kill them and then when she realized I wasn't going to, she acted like she wanted to lynch them. I'm afraid Pat wouldn't make a very good police officer."

The gas siphoners were the joke around the police department for the next few days. The patrolmen thought it was hilarious that the two dumb punks chose that apartment and that particular car for their little act. Mixed with the lighthearted ribbing, though, was an air of appreciation for the genuine coplike qualities of their Chief. His single-handed busts were becoming somewhat of a legend.

A few weeks before the gas siphoning incident,

Cochée personally busted what is called in cop jargon a "rolling GTA." In English it is an in-progress auto theft. (GTA: grand theft auto.)

"I was sitting at a red light and I spotted this new white Buick that was approaching the intersection from the cross street," Cochée recalled. "The driver was acting really strange, like he didn't want to catch the green light. There were two guys in the car, and they were both looking at me. They had spotted my unmarked car. They almost stopped, trying to catch the red light—I guess so that I would have to go ahead of them—but they finally turned right. When my light turned green I proceeded through the intersection and got behind them. They went slow and I went slow. They picked up speed and I picked up speed. Pretty soon they were really speeding, and I had a chase going. They were skidding around turns and I was trying to stay with them—without killing myself or somebody else—and at the same time I was giving a running commentary on our position so that a patrol car could cut them off. But I hadn't really learned the streets in town yet, and most of the time I didn't know where I was.

"Finally, they pulled into an alley and started climbing out of the car. I pulled up behind them and the two guys from the front seat were already out and halfway down the alley. Then I saw a guy in the backseat trying to get out. As he came out of the car I put my gun to his head. He froze.

"I shook him down and finally a backup unit arrived. We discovered only then that another guy—a friend of theirs—had been sitting in a nearby parked car, watching the entire scene. I must have had my back to him for five minutes without knowing it. Jesus, that was dangerous."

• • •

Los Angeles County Coroner's autopsy report:

"The body is identified by a toe tap. It is that of an embalmed female stated to be 22 years of age and appearing to be as stated. The body weighs 140 lbs. and measures 64 inches. The hair is black. The irises are brown. Identifying marks are elsewhere recorded.

"There is advanced decomposition. Skin peeling is apparent over almost the entire trunk and upper arms. The face and tongue are bloated and the abdomen is distended.

"Entrance wound: the left side of the neck anteriorly. A large gaping hole 5 ½ cm. in diameter is seen in the left neck. Its inner margin extends across the midline to the right. Its edges are soft and liquefied.

"Exit wound: none.

"The direction: straight.

"The penetration: the left clavicle and first rib are shattered. The left upper lobe is fragmented. The blood vessels in this region are lacerated.

"Missile is recovered. Three wads and multiple pellets are recovered from this region."

In medical terms, so ended the life of Margaret Johnson. She was blasted at close range with a 12-gauge shotgun at 11 P.M. on the night of January 5, 1973. She is described in the police record as FNA: female Negro adult. She was 22 years of age. The murderer has not yet been apprehended. It has now been more than two months since the murder and in police jargon the case is "cold." But two detectives have been given permission to work overtime on a Saturday to review the case and find a suspect.

Detective John Soisson is the pride of Compton's homicide division. He is white, in his late thirties, with a slightly paunchy look. Professionally there is nothing paunchy about him. In short, he is a maniac for details. He pores over evidence and details and reports verbally, announcing them to his partner as if to see how they sound, then he pores over them again; each time coming up with some new minute connection that may or may not mean anything.

In 1972, when Compton was the scene of 45 homicides, Soisson was personally responsible for all the follow-up investigations. He cleared (or solved) 41 of them; a phenomenal rate when one considers that the Los Angeles Police Department has a homicide investigator with a 60% clearance rate who is reputed to be one of the best detectives in the country. The end of 1973, however, a departmental administrator (a captain) decided that all homicide investigations would be divided equally among all the detectives, in order to give all of them homicide experience. It is a policy that Soisson is bitter about. The clearance rate has dropped and, as will be described herewith in the Margaret Johnson investigation, for good reason.

Detective Thomas Barclay was previously assigned to the gang detail (he was the Hoss-like white officer who walked into the middle of the marching gang in my magazine story). He was shifted to homicide when the captain in charge kept complaining to the Chief about how short-handed he was in the detective division. Barclay, who is only on loan to detectives from the Chief's Office, hopes someday to go back to gangs. In the meantime, he fears that not being on the street continuously will lose him some of his valuable contacts that he worked so hard to establish. He is obviously happy to be teamed with the professional Soisson for this case, but he too is upset with the present homicide investigation policy, and lets it be known.

"The body was badly bloated because it wasn't found until four days after the shooting," Barclay explained. "Margaret didn't smell good at all. . . . She apparently opened the door at 11 o'clock at night dressed only in panties, bra, and short nightie. A friend said she would never have answered the door like that unless it was someone she knew. But that's nothing, 90% of all homicides are committed by people who know the victims. . . . From the angle of the wound, she must have been killed with a sawed-off shotgun while she was kneeling on the floor, either begging for her life or sucking some guy's joint. Otherwise, for her to have been shot with a full-length shotgun, the guy would have had to be standing on furniture shooting down at her. I think it was an execution-type slaying with a sawed-off."

Margaret was no angel. She was obviously seeing many guys—young and old. She was always behind in her rent and was "dating" the middle-aged, white slumlord who didn't push quite as hard for his back rent after their first "date." In a strange dichotomy of character, she was also a Jesus Freak. Among her personal possessions found in the small house were several handwritten religious poems asking for forgiveness and beseeching humanity to absolve itself of its sins. Also found were: an application for a job-training program (she was unemployed); a three-week old notice from the gas and electric company that her service had been turned off for nonpayment; two letters from the horny landlord, and several pictures, including one of Margaret herself dressed in a stylish black-and-white checkered dress, looking young and pretty. Barclay, who had already shown me the horrible pictures of the dead body, said, "Can you believe this was the same person?"

Yes, I could, but not without a feeling of nausea. For some insanely morbid reason I kept studying the death pictures, as if they would tell me something about Margaret or her killer. She was lying on her stomach in the corner of her living room, as if she had backed away from the assailant as he she came toward her. When she was shot and fell face-forward, her feet had kicked over a large flower vase on the floor, and the big, leafy plant draped grotesquely over the body.

In the pictures taken by the police in the coroner's examining room before the autopsy, the body was stretched out on a stainless steel table. One picture showed her on her back, her body bloated, her braless breasts bulging in death. In another picture, this one a side frontal view, her panties had been cut away and her belly looked obscenely inflated. Then there was a picture from behind, with her swollen buttocks overpowering all other features. The wound itself was the worst. From the neck up Margaret looked like a ball of raw, brownish meat; a patch of black hair strangely growing on top. Her face was a massive, angry, open scab. Facial features such as the eyes and mouth were barely recognizable. Remembering that another human being had purposely inflicted this kind of cruel, ugly, bloody death upon Margaret made me shudder. I decided then and there that I would dog Soisson and Barclay as they investigated this case. And hopefully, I would be on the scene when they cracked this one wide open.

3

CHASING TURKEY

"If you really want to find out what's going on around here, ride with the troopies."

– Patrolman Robert Oroscoe, Compton P.D.

I had a gut feeling after observing from afar several other city police departments that the backbone of a police force is its patrol division. There is no doubt that this is the segment of police work that is most exciting. At various times it is also satisfying and frustrating. On patrol you confront the people face to face. They can be law-abiding citizens who are pleased to see you patrolling their neighborhoods or they can be armed hoods in the progress of committing a felony who want to get away, even if they have to kill you to do it. In either case, you are standing there in the uniform and badge, representing The Law. And you are terribly vulnerable.

Friday night in Compton is the best time to be a "ride-along" on patrol, for the chances of something major coming down are slightly better than even money. After having a Friday night dinner at Tom and Pat Cochée's apartment, I asked Tom to take me back to the station so I could pick up a ride with a patrol car. Then, once we were at the station, I asked Tom to take me into the beat commander's office and introduce me. It was only natural that I use Tom as an emissary, because I hadn't yet gone on patrol here. But it was the last time I asked him to do that. After Tom left, the sergeant went to communications and asked what car was available. Radio said that a car was due in any minute to drop off a prisoner, and the sergeant told me that I could catch a ride with it. A few minutes later, the sergeant took me into the squad room, and I was introduced to Officer Robert Oroscoe.

"This is Bruce Henderson, a friend of the Chief's."

Oroscoe looked up momentarily from the typewriter he was using to bang out an arrest report, but gave no recognition that I was sucking oxygen in the same room with him.

The sergeant continued to torpedo me: "He's going to be riding with you tonight. So clean up your act, Oroscoe, or he'll report you to the Chief."

Oh, shit. How am I ever going to overcome this, I wondered. Oroscoe looked up at me again, and this time his large brown eyes said: "Screw you, you ass-kisser!"

The sergeant left, and I was alone in the room with Mr. Warmth. Very few times in my life have I felt more self-conscious. As my eyes nervously darted back and forth across the room—trying desperately not to get caught looking at him—I checked him out.

Robert Oroscoe was a short, stocky, light-complexed Mexican with a thin moustache and a jovial, round face. Although only in his mid-twenties, he already had the beginnings of a beer-drinking paunch. Unbelievably, as I looked him over, I had the feeling that despite his obvious hostility toward me now, we could hit it off if we ever got to know each other. (After all, if I were in his position, I probably wouldn't treat too kindly a fink friend of the Chief's.) Of all the people I had met so far on the department, I felt this was the guy I could get to know as a friend the easiest. There's something unsettling about that: how I either turn on or off to someone just based on the initial chemistry between us, which may or may not have anything to do with the words spoken. I mean, I could already see myself guzzling beer with this irreverent son of a bitch. All I had to do was get past that incredible introduction. I decided that a bold move was needed.

"Look, in case you're wondering, I'm writing a book on this department," I finally blurted.

"Is the book for or against the department?" he asked quickly, barely looking up from the typewriter.

"Depends on what I see," I told him. "But I'm impressed by what I've seen of the Chief's attitude on law enforcement."

He seemed to sink.

"But I'm not a press agent," I added.

"Okay," he said with genuine finality.

Mainly as a diversion I inserted a piece of paper into a nearby typewriter and began writing up some notes I had stored in my head. In a few minutes another officer walked into the room and Oroscoe looked up from the typewriter.

"Hey, how do you spell deceased?" Oroscoe asked the other officer. Then, not waiting for an answer, he said: "Oh, shit, I'll just put down that the fucker croaked."

• • •

In the security parking lot behind the police building, Oroscoe and reserve officer Messerle checked out the patrol car as I tried to get comfortable in the backseat. (Like most major departments, Compton utilizes reserves to beef up their units to two-man cars. The reserves buy their own uniforms, get no pay, and are required to qualify regularly on the shooting range and put in a certain number of hours on patrol each month. Many reserves are attending college and plan to go into law enforcement work eventually, but others just do it for community service or to get their jollies off.) The patrol car they began the night with developed radio trouble, so they were assigned another unit. While checking out the lights and siren and washing the windows, Oroscoe complained loudly about the overall condition of the city's police cars.

"If you weren't a friend of the Chief's I'd tell you about these patrol cars!" Oroscoe spat.

"Go ahead and tell me anyway," I said firmly, getting pissed at the VIP treatment.

"Okay," Oroscoe said without hesitation. "They have no police suspension, 10-year-old radios that are always going off frequency, two-barrel carburetors . . . every punk in town knows he can outrun us. So they always try. . . . This is our second car tonight, and that's not uncommon. Usually half the cars in this lots are down with some mechanical failure."

Oroscoe and Messerle buckled their seat belts and I tried to find mine.

"You have to lift up the seat to get the belt," Oroscoe said. "You want me to do it?"

"No, don't worry about it."

We backed out of the parking place and weren't even clear of the lot before the radio barked out a call for us. A report of a shotgun shooting on a residential street. Code 3: Get your ass there as fast as you can, using red lights and siren. As I was to discover later, this is the code that allows policemen to become race-car drivers and speed in and out of traffic, sometimes on the wrong side of the street.

Oroscoe jumped on the accelerator and we bolted out of the lot, spun around a corner, and raced down a bumpy street that was under construction. The red lights bounced eerie reflections off the black night and the screaming siren cut a chilling tone. There's always been something about sirens at nighttime that completely destroys my psyche; all I can picture are scenes of tragedy, blood, violence. Somebody suffering. Somebody dying. It's scary as hell.

With every big chuckhole in the bumpy street my butt left the seat as the car's rear end fell out from under me. Each time my ass became airborne the top of my head hammered into the metal overhead. When we went over some elevated railroad tracks all four wheels left the ground and I felt like I'd just had an 80-pound bag of cement dropped on my noggin. In desperation I grabbed the riot helmet sitting on the seat beside me and quickly strapped it on. I looked up from my ordeal in time to see Oroscoe begin a long, slow-motion skid into a turn. He had wanted to make a high-speed turn onto a cross street without losing any momentum, but in the middle of his effort it felt as if he was going to lose it. He took his foot off the accelerator and touched the power brakes, and the wheels very nearly locked up.

"No!" Messerle yelled. "Stay on the gas! You got it!"

Oroscoe floored it again, and the power pulled us out of the mess. "Fuck!" Oroscoe yelled at no one in particular. "Fuck!"

Midway down the block several people were standing out on the sidewalk. This was a well-kept, lower middle-class neighborhood with nicely painted fences and mowed lawns. Porch lights were on and people were peering out windows and standing on porches and lawns. Something had obviously happened to disturb this cozy neighborhood. Oroscoe braked the car to stop adjacent to a group of adults standing on the sidewalk. We were the first car on the scene. Oroscoe and Messerle quickly jumped out.

"They just left," one man said excitedly. "They shot at that house over there."

"What kind of car are they driving?" Messerle asked.

"A Chevy pickup," the man answered.

Oroscoe and Messerle got back into the car. The trail was hot, and this was a bust they really wanted. Oroscoe turned the key and the ignition rattled for a second, then went dead. He tried it again, with the same result.

"Turn off the lights," Messerle said with a note of desperation in his voice. "We've got too much drain on the battery."

With everything shut down Oroscoe tried again. Nothing. Dead battery, dead generator, dead something. The neighbors peered nervously at the squad car, obviously wondering why we weren't going after the shotgun hoods. We sat disabled in the middle of the street. While Messerle called on the radio for a push, Oroscoe slumped behind the wheel like a lifeless puppet that just had its strings cut. "Compton's finest," he finally muttered. "This is fuckin' embarrassing."

In a few minutes another unit pulled up behind us. Messerle picked up the radio mike to talk directly to the other car. "Okay, give us a push." As the neighbors watched, we were pushed down the street, building up speed so that Oroscoe could drop it in gear and (hopefully) get the car running. At 20 miles per hour, Messerle said into the mike: "Faster." We got going to 25 mph before the other unit backed off. Oroscoe dropped it into second and we kept coasting, with no sound coming from under the hood.

"Take us around this corner," Messerle told the other unit. "Then get us going to 35. That's what we need to get it going."

Once around the corner the other unit began pushing us again. We were quickly up to 35. Nothing. One more try. This time, just as we were up to 35, a corner came up on us, and Oroscoe had to fight with the power steering and power brakes—which don't operate properly when the engine is off—in order to get us around the corner in one piece.

"Jesus, that's it," Oroscoe said. "Call for a tow."

The other unit left and we waited on a lonely darkened street, disabled.

Turning around to look at me, Oroscoe said sourly: "See what I mean about these cars? This is dangerous, sitting here like this in the area of a known shooting. We couldn't even get the shotgun out of its holder." (The bracket snaps open on a signal from a button under the dash but the engine must be running to activate the mechanism.) "And the radio, our lifeline, is slowly draining."

In about 15 minutes a tow truck pulled up and the driver jumped our lifeless battery with his truck's. Our engine started immediately. As the tow truck left, Messerle firmly cautioned Oroscoe: "For Christ's sake, don't turn the key off."

"Say, before we get back on the road," I said, "I think I'd like to find that seat belt."

We weren't back on patrol 10 minutes before the radio directed us to a 459 at a gas station. This is another winner: a silent burglary alarm has gone off. Possible burglary in progress. No lights or siren are used on this call, because the cops don't want to give the hoods any warning. Oroscoe is making the car move again, but this time being extra careful because other drivers don't have the warning of his red lights and siren. We went down a side street, then onto Compton Boulevard, toward an unlit gas station on the corner. We pulled across the street and drove onto the station lot. A car was parked next to the station's rest rooms, and two men were sitting in the car; one on the passenger's side and the other in the backseat. Oroscoe pulled the patrol car up in front of the car, leaving about 18 feet between the two vehicles. Messerle got on the radio, giving Communications the car's license number in order to run a warrant check (and also to keep on record in case they are shot on this stop).

Suddenly another man stepped out of the men's room. Oroscoe hit him with the beam of the unit's high-powered spotlight. The man didn't even flinch—almost as if he was expecting us. He calmly walked to the car and got into the driver's seat. The light went back to the restroom door. The coin box on the door had been pried off, and was missing.

Messerle opened his door first. He had already taken his .357 magnum out of his holster and was holding it in his right hand, down at his side. He began to approach the car slowly, walking wide to the right. If he had to dive for cover the station building was only a few feet away.

Oroscoe opened his door then. He didn't take his gun out, but he had his hand on the stock, ready to whip it out of his fast-draw holster. He made a wide half-circle to the left, but as he approached the car he had no cover whatsoever. If only one man in the car had a weapon and decided to use it at that moment—and if he was a halfway decent shot—Robert Oroscoe and possibly Messerle would be dead. Oroscoe for sure. Messerle maybe.

I watched all this from the backseat of the patrol car. My adrenaline was pumping viciously; I was scared shitless for them. I knew that Oroscoe and Messerle were scared, too, and felt the same adrenaline surge. They would have to be robots not to. This was what being a cop came down to: this kind of night-felon-stop confrontation. This was where these guys put everything on the line.

When the two officers reached the car, they ordered the three men, all blacks in their mid-twenties, out of the vehicle. The men got out passively, carefully holding their hands above their heads. As Messerle watched them,

Oroscoe went into the rest room. He came out a minute later, and nodded at Messerle. A backup unit pulled up, then a few seconds later the beat sergeant arrived. Oroscoe led the sergeant into the rest room as the men were handcuffed and put into another patrol car.

I had climbed out of the backseat once the other units were on the scene. (Brave journalist.) I stood a few feet away from the suspects' car, which was being thoroughly searched. The sergeant and Oroscoe came out of the rest room, and Oroscoe motioned for me to come over. I followed him into the rest room. With his flashlight illuminating the pitch-black space, Oroscoe pointed out the broken coin box lying in the small garbage can, a crowbar, and a bag of dimes.

"See that nice print on the coin box?" Oroscoe said. "If that comes out, we can make it stick on that guy."

"What did he tell you he was doing?"

"Oh, he said he just stopped by to take a shit. Didn't know nothin' else."

"Just sitting here taking a shit in the dark, huh?"

"Yeah," Oroscoe said.

"You really made a good bust," I said.

"You think so?"

"Hell yes. You caught 'em cold."

"A smart lawyer can get them off," Oroscoe declared. "First of all, the two guys sitting in the car are out of the picture. Even though they knew damn well what their buddy was doing, we can't prove they were accessories."

"What about the dude who came strutting out of here?" I protested.

"Well, I know damn well what happened," Oroscoe said, still pointing the light at the bag of coins. "He stepped out with the stuff and spotted us coming down Compton Boulevard, so he just came back in here and dumped everything. Then he came walking out like nothing happened. But I'll show you what a good attorney will do to me on the witness stand:

"Defense: 'Now, officer, was the restroom well-lit?'

" 'No sir.'

" 'Was it dark?'

" 'Yes, sir.'

" 'What did you see there, without using your flashlight?'

" 'Well, it was dark. I used my flashlight.'

" 'I see. What did you see with your flashlight on?'

" 'In the wastebasket there was a broken coin box and what appeared to be a crowbar.'

" 'But the defendant didn't have a flashlight, did he?'

"' No, sir.'

" 'Now, officer, could the defendant, if he wasn't looking for those things in the trash can, have walked by it in the dark on the way to relieving himself?'

" 'Yes, sir, he could have. But . . .'

" 'No more questions.' "

Oroscoe was through with his very real playacting, and I was slightly shaken. I felt as if I'd just lost my first bust. When we walked from the rest room, the suspects had already been taken to the station. Oroscoe and Messerle now had to wait at the scene until the special investigative unit (S.I.) arrived to take pictures and gather the evidence.

"I've got to tell you guys, that was really a hairy thing watching you approach that car like that," I admitted.

"We were wide open," Oroscoe admitted. "If I had it

to do over again, I would have yelled for the guys to have gotten out of the car one at a time, while we stayed near the car. But, you know, that's what happens. You make so many of these stops that you get brave, or careless. Then, the next time you do it, you get wasted."

"Why did you get out of the car first?" I asked Messerle.

"Because I happen to like this fat Mexican," he said only half-joking. "We've worked together so much that we just automatically know what the other person should do. I didn't have to tell him what I was doing. He knew. And I knew he'd be out right behind me."

As we waited in the darkened station, the three of us had no problem conversing. The initial hostility that Oroscoe had shown me had disappeared. For some reason we were almost like partners; maybe because we had gone through a night felony bust together.

"Why do you think this guy put a silent alarm on his toilets?" I asked.

"Probably because his coin boxes have been ripped off before," Messerle answered.

"A lousy bag of dimes," I said. "How old were these guys?"

"They were all 28 or 29, and had Hollywood addresses," Oroscoe said.

"Couldn't have been more than five or 10 bucks in that bag," I said. "They came all the way from Hollywood for that?"

"Yeah, well, that's probably 10 bucks more than they had," Oroscoe said. "If they knock off five or ten stations a night, that would get them a little bread. The word gets around, too. They think Compton is an easy score because the police are too busy."

Oroscoe moved to the suspects' car that was still parked next to the station, waiting for the police tow truck to haul it away, too. The car was a two- or three-year-old purple Pontiac with wide tires and mag wheels. Oroscoe flipped the ignition key on and the stereo tape machine came on loudly, filling the night with vibrating rock music.

"Shit, burglars drive nice cars like this and I drive an old VW," Oroscoe said disgustedly as he looked over the nicely upholstered interior. He tapped his hand on the dashboard, keeping time to the music.

"You know, I can really see how you feel," I admitted. "I'm a strong believer in individual and human rights, and I think it's incumbent upon the cop to make a legal arrest without breaking any constitutional laws, but to lose one like this. . . . Shit, it was so obvious to us here on the scene. But it can be made to seem much different in a court of law."

"I'll tell you something you won't believe," Oroscoe said, turning off the music. He got out of the car and leaned against the station wall. "The landmark case on juveniles being allowed to talk to their parents in private after they are arrested—just like an adult's right to talk to an attorney—came out of Compton. A kid held up a grocery store here and killed the Mom and Pop owners, who were about 70 years old. When he was arrested he asked to speak to his father, but was told that since his father wasn't an attorney he couldn't. He then confessed to the killings. Later, the Supreme Court overruled the conviction, saying that juveniles have the right to talk in private with their parents. The kid was in jail for three years, then back out on the street.

"Not long ago, a kid shot another kid for no reason. He told us: 'Just 'cause I wanted to.' But the court overturned his conviction because when he spoke to his father it was in a room from which the conversation could be heard in the next room. So there he was, out on the streets proudly telling everybody that he got away with murder because his rights had been violated.

"The thing that really pisses me off is that we keep busting the same people and they keep coming back on the streets again after serving little or no time.

"Then they wonder why we have a high crime rate."

When the S.I. unit arrived to gather the evidence, the patrolman was accompanied by a pretty, black female reserve officer. Oroscoe immediately threw his arms around the young woman.

"Why didn't you wear your short dress tonight?" a disappointed Oroscoe asked.

"I didn't want to turn you on again," she responded.

"Say, zip your zipper up," Messerle instructed Oroscoe.

"What you doin' noticing?" said Oroscoe, as he took the S.I. officer into the rest room to show him what pictures to take of the evidence.

I moved next to the woman reserve, with my notebook in hand. "Say, why do you want to be a cop?"

"Because it's my life," she said sarcastically.

After a few minutes, Messerle, who had been waiting outside with us, rapped on the restroom door. "Hey, save some for me," he yelled.

When Oroscoe finally came out, Messerle said impatiently: "Goddammit, zip your zipper up!"

Oroscoe looked down sheepishly and tugged the zipper up. "It's only down a little."

"Man, you got zipper on the mind," the woman reserve said to Messerle.

Patrolman Robert Oroscoe and partner "jack up" gang members for routine "field interrogations."

Oroscoe empties pockets of one of the many persons he had brought into

jail during a long night.

Oroscoe's final decision in a family fight: handcuffs and an arrest of the alleged abuser.

I spent the next night on patrol with 24-year-old John Wilkinson, a tall, slender, white patrolman who had been with the department for three years. The first hour of his shift he was assigned an unmarked detectives' car. It was more underpowered than the underpowered patrol cars and in worse general condition. It would be an hour before a black-and-white unit would be available, but Wilkinson was so disgusted with the unmarked car that we hid out in a coffee shop. He was determined not to be caught out in public with it. "Hell, what kind of image is that?"

Unlike many of the Compton officers I had spoken with, Wilkinson did not hold in utter disregard the former police chief, a sickly white man in his sixties who had retired prior to Cochée being hired. The reason was that Wilkinson's mother had just recently retired from the department—after serving the last 15 years or so as the old chief's personal secretary. Indeed, the former chief had become a close family friend.

Wilkinson's parents, who were both retired, still lived in Compton. John, a bachelor, resided with them. "I'd like to have an apartment in another city," Wilkinson admitted. "But I'm staying with my parents to protect them. Before I moved back in with them, they were having trouble with the punks in the neighborhood. Once I moved back, though, word got around that a cop lived there and we haven't had any trouble since. I'll stay with my parents until they sell their house and move. Which I hope is pretty soon."

Wilkinson became a cop because he needed a job. "The money was good," he said, "so I decided why not. I hadn't really figured on becoming a cop, but that's how things worked out."

After drinking coffee for an hour, we drove back to the police station. While I waited outside in the parking lot, Wilkinson went into the station to pick up the keys to a black-and-white unit. In a few minutes he came out with another uniformed officer.

"This is Jack McConnell," Wilkinson said. "Jack's going to go Code 7 with us." (Code 7: We are going to dinner.)

Officer Jack McConnell, a large-boned, overweight,

pale-faced, redheaded Irishman, shook hands with me absentmindedly. When Wilkinson told him I was working on a book, McConnell perked up. "A book on police procedures or what?" he questioned.

"Actually, I'm going to emphasize the people more than the procedures," I said.

"On a lot of departments?"

"No, just this one," I said.

"Why did you pick us ?" McConnell asked as he eyed me suspiciously.

"I know the Chief, and last fall I came down here to do a magazine story on him," I explained. "I decided that what was going on here would make a good book."

"Did you tell him about the racial stuff?" McConnell asked Wilkinson.

"No," Wilkinson said.

"Guess I'd better keep my mouth shut, too," McConnell said. "You'll find out soon enough."

It didn't take much persuasion to change McConnell's mind about keeping his mouth shut. During the course of a spicy meal at the best Mexican restaurant in town, McConnell unleashed an embittered tirade directed at Chief Cochée's salt-and-pepper directive. Recognizing that most ghetto riots have been touched off by the actions of white police officers working in black neighborhoods, the Chief ordered that all two-man patrol units would henceforth be integrated. McConnell claimed that the order was blatantly prejudicial. He said that since every patrol shift has more black officers than whites, the result is that two whites can never again go on patrol together, although two blacks can. Apparently the order broke up some long-time teams, including the all-white team of

McConnell and Officer Dolf Wagner.

Wagner, a soft-spoken, amiable, 35-year-old man with prematurely gray hair, didn't fight the order. But McConnell, with a quick and vocal Irish temper and disposition, made his feelings known to the world. Consequently, he was no longer on patrol. Ever since the blowup, he had been working radio communications—and sorely missing street duty.

"Look, people who hate cops just hate cops, period," McConnell told me. "They don't hate you because you are white or black, they just hate you because you are a cop."

"Okay," I said, "but aren't there possible situations in a city like Compton, with such a large black population, in which you would like to have a black partner along?"

"No. Why?"

"Just for survival," I argued. "You get a call involving a black gang fight, and if two white cops pull up, that could be real trouble. I mean, you would be The Man."

"There are black officers on this department who I would never want to work with under any circumstance," McConnell said. "And there are some white officers on this department who scare me to death. . . . We have racist cops in this department. Whites and blacks. We all know who they are. And they should never ride together. But just to divide up all the white officers because they are white is unfair."

Unfortunately, the inflections in McConnell's voice during this conversation do not come through in print. It's important for me to point out that these remarks were offered in heated and challenging tones. Several times I felt that I was conversing with a man who had a monumental chip on his shoulder. There was something else about Jack McConnell that I couldn't quite put my finger on. He had something pent up inside him, fighting to get out. With the fervor with which he spoke, I had the feeling that he was a human bomb ready to explode.

On the ride back to the station to drop McConnell off for his radio duties, Wilkinson, who had been almost totally silent during the dinner conversation, drove the patrol car and McConnell sat in the front seat beside him. I sat in the back directly behind McConnell, and watched the back of his head as he talked.

"I'm 28 years old and have been married for 10 years," McConnell said. "Cops should never be married. You see, I always wanted to be the best damn patrolman in this department, and to work at a job that hard you have to sacrifice other things—like your family. I have a high-school education. Never went to college. I don't think you have to be educated to be a cop. You just have to have a feeling for the job, and a desire to be the best. I miss being on patrol. That was my life.

"I don't know why I stay here. I could go to L.A.S.O. (Los Angeles County Sheriff's Office) and make more money, drive newer cars, and have pump shotguns. Well, I'm not going to stay much longer. They can have it. . . . They are discriminating against my race, and I don't like it."

McConnell was quiet for a moment, as if he was fed up with talking. As we drove through an intersection, several young blacks were lurking on the corner, obviously not going anywhere, and neatly fitting the term "corner brothers" that I first heard from a black friend.

"Look at these punks on the corner," McConnell

said with genuine ferocity in his voice. "Just shuckin' and jivin', waiting to rip off the decent people. . . . You know why cops just hang around with other cops? Because they are suspicious of everyone else. You get so you can't stand anyone who's not a cop. All you see is the seamy side of life. All the worst fuckers in the world.

"Shit, I'm getting so I hate people."

• • •

An hour after dinner, Wilkinson is trying to explain to me why he needs to write more traffic citations even though there isn't a quota per se on how many he has to write in a month. I had just finished observing that in my 18 or so hours riding patrol in this city, I had yet to see a policeman write a traffic ticket. It had seemed to me that the cops here were too busy to stop someone for driving seven miles an hour over the posted speed limit.

"If you stay with me the rest of the night, you'll see some citations written," Wilkinson promised. "I need some bad."

"You mean you have a quota?" I said.

"I don't tend to write too many, and last month I only wrote three," he explained. "The Captain issued a directive asking why some officers wrote only a few tickets last month. Really, it's best to write about 10 to 20 a month. Then no questions are asked. The city gets pissed off because citations mean money."

Ten minutes later a car passed us in the opposite direction on a residential street, and the driver kept his high-beam lights on when he went by us. What normally might have resulted in a warning from Officer Wilkinson resulted instead in a citation.

"I have a way of selling tickets so that the people don't get up tight," Wilkinson said as he wrote out the citation on the hood of the patrol car, under the bright light of the spotlight. The driver, a middle-aged black man, came back to the patrol car and signed his ticket. He was not up tight, but he definitely wasn't overjoyed either. I felt like whispering to him that Wilkinson really wasn't a bad guy, and in fact he lets a lot of motorists off without tickets, but this month he really needs some bad. But somehow I didn't think the guy would have appreciated it.

•   •   •

Sometime later we were parked next to a closed service station and Wilkinson was filling out two pages of paper work on a routine, noninjury fender-bender that involved a hit-and-run driver. Suddenly, Jack McConnell's voice came over the air in a jarring tone. In the last couple of hours I had noted that McConnell handled his radio dispatch duties in a dispassionate voice, typical of the police radio voice that betrays no emotion. But this time was different.

"Code 9. Code 3. Pine and 9th."

(Code 9: Officer needs help. Code 3: Desperately.)

Wilkinson threw aside his paper work, flipped on the red light and siren and stepped on the accelerator. We peeled rubber out of the gas station and jumped into moderate traffic on Compton Boulevard, a main thoroughfare with two lanes of traffic in each direction, separated in many places by concrete islands. Wilkinson seemingly had his accelerator foot on the floor, and as we gained on some cars in the right lane that were traveling at normal speeds, Wilkinson swiftly steered us into the left lane and we were still accelerating as we zoomed by them.

McConnell's voice boomed over the radio again: "Shots fired at officers." His voice clearly cracked with emotion this time. Jack McConnell wanted to be out on the street, speeding to the aid of his fellow officers, instead of trapped in the helplessness of the communications center.

We were approaching cars from behind, and none of them were moving over to the right. We were going so fast now that we seemed to suck up the sound of our own siren; I could barely hear it myself. As for the red lights, a driver ahead would have to look in the rear-view mirror to see them. Unfortunately, most drivers don't check the rear-view mirror every 30 seconds, so we were really picking up on them. Wilkinson cussed loudly: "Fucker! Move over! Goddammit!" At a break in the islands, Wilkinson swerved the patrol car onto the other side of the concrete structure, and we raced down the wrong side of the street. Traffic ahead of us was stopped at a red light, and when the light changed to green they stayed where they were. Unlike the people we came up on from behind, these people saw our red lights, and they froze on the spot. I looked at the speedometer for the first time. It read 90 mph. I straightened my body out, placing my feet squarely on the firewall and stiffening my back so that if (or when) we got into an accident I would be able to absorb much of the shock in my legs. The seat belt gripped me tightly, and that gave me a feeling of security, until I remembered reading medical reports about internal organs being seriously damaged from seat belts cutting into the body on high-speed accidents.

Wilkinson deftly whipped the car back into the right lane of traffic at the intersection at which the cars going toward us were stopped cold in their tracks. We missed the concrete island and steel power pole by inches. This is fucking ridiculous, I thought. First of all, what good are we going to be to the guys being shot at if we get killed in a traffic accident ? Secondly, why the hell should I get killed? All I want to do is write a book. As I watched us eating up the street in front of us, it occurred to me that 90 miles an hour never seemed so fast before. Shit, I go 90 on the highway sometimes. But here, on this street, dodging these assholes who don't see us coming, it is downright crazy. Then up ahead a car from a cross street pulled out in front of us, trying to merge into traffic going the other direction. It sat in the roadway, blocking us. Even if Wilkinson stood on the brakes now, we would slam into it at a terrific speed. We were dead. That's all there was to it. I would die in Compton, while researching my first book. I shut my eyes.

The wheels squealed on the street, but they clearly weren't the noise of Wilkinson hitting the brakes. No, he was trying to steer us out of the fatal accident. The rear end first skidded to the left, then to the right, and when I opened my eyes our target was gone. We had missed it. I didn't even have time to feel relieved, because the very next moment we were again on the other side of the island, and this time the cars coming at us head-on were not stopped at a red light. They were coming toward us, desperately trying to move over to the right. Just as we were seriously threatening to ram head-first into the oncoming traffic, Wilkinson stood on the brakes, and turned the wheel to the left. Our rear end slid to the right, and Wilkinson stepped on the accelerator, propelling us off the boulevard and onto a side street. We slowed down to 60 mph on the narrow street, and finally navigated another skidding turn. Up ahead were two patrol cars with red lights flashing parked in the middle of the street. Wilkinson jumped out and disappeared into a house, where a party was obviously in progress. Within 60 seconds there were two other backup units on the scene. A handcuffed young Mexican man was brought out of the house and placed in the backseat of a unit. The police had also apprehended the weapon that had been used to fire the shots. (In attendance at the party were dozens of young Mexicans.) The cops suspected there were other weapons around, but a cursory inspection revealed nothing.

There was no doubt that I was still in a strange state of shock. I was shaking and felt weak in the legs, and my nerves seemed to be shattered forever. Actually, over the years I have enjoyed high-speed driving at times when I have a clear open road in front of me. But the speeding ride I had just survived through city traffic was the most harrowing of my life. Just minutes before we began our wild chase Wilkinson had been telling me that high-speed chases are a very powerful emotional experience; something that is hard to get used to, no matter how many times you do it. He said that after police officers chase a suspect through town at high speeds and finally nab the guy, he is usually roughed up pretty good.

"After you've chased some turkey at 90 or 100 miles

an hour and put your life on the line, you just don't handle him too gently," Wilkinson said. "He usually gets beat on."

To me it sounded like police brutality. But I have to admit that if I had to make an arrest, handcuff someone, and put him in the back of my car after that incredible race across town, I wouldn't have done it too kindly. I was completely on edge. And our race didn't even have a protagonist in front of us, trying to get away. In that case, when you finally get a hold of the guy, you must feel like a defensive tackle who has been beaten all day but who finally, in the closing minutes of the fourth quarter, gets his hands around the neck of the opposing quarterback. The temptation is just too great.

"Were you always a fast driver?" I asked Wilkinson after we had resumed our patrol.

"Oh, God, no," he said. "I always drove like an old lady. I always had old cars anyway, and I just crept along slower than the rest of the traffic."

"Was it hard to learn—driving that fast?"

Wilkinson smiled. "My training officer was an old-timer named Pat Dempsey. He works detectives now. It was the very first night he let me drive that I got my first Code Nine call. I started rolling along at 40 or 50, and Dempsey said for me to step on it. I picked it up to 60 or 70, and Dempsey yelled: 'Put your foot on the floor and don't let up until we get there.' My foot went on the floor and I didn't let up.

"Later, Dempsey told me that when an officer on this or any department needs help, I will roll as fast as I can. He said if ever I didn't, he would personally kick my ass."

Fact: Two Compton police officers were rolling on a Code 9-Code 3 last year, tearing ass down a city street when they collided with a slow-moving car that pulled out in front of them from a cross street. The teen-age boy who was driving the car was killed instantly. One of the officers struck his head on the shotgun and was in the hospital for several days for a concussion.

Chief Cochée is not at all happy about balls-to-the-wall responses to Officer Needs Help calls. "They don't do anybody any good if they get into an accident on the way," he explained. "I want them to slow down. Needless to say, it's a very touchy subject with the officer. But I'm going to have to do something about it."

• • •

A few minutes after midnight a screaming woman hailed our patrol car from the porch of a small, rundown house. Wilkinson stopped the car and backed up in front of the house and broadcast over the radio that he was getting out of the car to assist a screaming woman. A Code Nine would be in order.

It was a young, slender, once-attractive black woman who was drunk and/or stoned and was acting like an incoherent fool. She was babbling about "my baby . . . ohh, they have my baby," pointing to the house.

"Who has your baby?" Wilkinson asked.

"They do!" she muttered. "Won't . . . give me . . . my baby."

By now a middle-aged black woman was standing in the doorway of the dimly lit house, watching Wilkinson and the woman. There appeared to be several other adults and children in the living room.

Wilkinson obviously wasn't too anxious to go into the house alone, but finally he said, "Okay, let's go get your baby."

While Wilkinson went in the house, I waited outside next to the patrol car. He wasn't in the house more than a minute before I heard squealing tires and turned to see a black-and-white unit making a sweeping, speedy turn around the nearby corner. This is our backup. While the driver got out and joined Wilkinson in the house—motioning for me to come with him—the other officer in the two-man car stayed outside by the radio, just in case.

Policemen consider family-disturbance calls the worst situations to go in to. Statistics support their contention, as studies show that more policemen are killed on these types of interventions than anything else. A family can be fighting or even killing each other, but often when a policeman comes in he is viewed as an outsider, and seen as a threat to loved ones who just seconds ago were kicking or mutilating each other. Suddenly the policeman becomes the target for an insane, misplaced hostility.

Inside the house there was much yelling, and the two women started at each other several times. Neither patrolman was anxious to jump in the middle and have his eyes scratched out, but somehow a fight was avoided and the small child, a girl of five or six, was brought out of the house with her mother.

"These women are friends," Wilkinson explained to me, "and the older one didn't think the young one was in the condition to take her kid home with her. So she was going to keep the girl for the night. The thing is, they might be screaming at each other tonight, but tomorrow they'll again be the best of friends."

Once Wilkinson got the woman and her child out on the sidewalk, the backup unit left for another call. Now Wilkinson was the one who wanted to make sure the woman was in condition to handle herself and her child. He told her to roll up her long sleeves. When she did, he flashed the light on her arms and studied her skin.

"You used to be on it, huh, Patty?"

"Been a long time," she slurred.

"Yeah, I can see that. What are you on now?"

"Nothin. I'm clean. Been long time."

Wilkinson flashed the light in her eyes, to check the pupil response. "Look," he said, "I'm going to let you go, but I want you to go right home. If you come back here tonight I'm going to take you to jail. You understand that?"

The woman nodded.

Wilkinson looked at the little girl, who was rubbing her eyes and seemed thoroughly confused by the night's events.

"You tired, honey," he said, patting her head.

The little girl looked up at Wilkinson with chocolate-brown eyes and nodded her head slowly.

"Okay, Patty, you take your little girl home and put her to bed," said Wilkinson. "Go on now."

He watched as the woman and girl walked down the street, then turned the corner.

"She used to be a heroin user. She's got plenty of old tracks. Now she's high on reds. I could have taken her in, but she wasn't that bad. I just want to see that little girl get off the street and home to bed."

Six blocks away, Wilkinson spotted two young boys ducking around a corner when they saw the patrol car. He turned the corner and stopped in the middle of the street. A young boy of 12 or 13 was standing next to a garage with his hands in his pockets, trying to act cool. His buddy had taken a fence and was long gone. But Mr. Cool obviously thought he could jive this cop.

Wilkinson waved him over to the patrol car. The boy approached the car on my side, and I rolled down my window.

"What are you doing?" Wilkinson demanded.

"I'm just walking, man."

"Walking where?"

The youngster shrugged his shoulders.

"Where do you live?"

The boy mumbled something. Ah, the old mumble-the-address-trick. Wilkinson bolted out of the car and went around to the other side of the car. He opened the back door and motioned the boy into the backseat. Slamming the door shut, Wilkinson got back behind the wheel.

"What you got me for?" the boy exclaimed, betraying some panic in his voice.

"For sucking up too much air," Wilkinson said firmly.

After driving for a couple of minutes, Wilkinson finally said, "Okay, where do you live?"

This time the boy crisply gave his address, and Wilkinson drove to the house. He pulled up in front of the house and took the boy out from the backseat. A man came out on the porch of the boy's house and yelled: "Don't tell 'em who I am! Don't tell 'em nothing about me!"

Wilkinson emptied the boy's pockets on the hood of the car, carefully examining everything. Then he began filling out an F.I. card—field interrogation card, which would give the boy's name, address and description and go on file at the police station so other officers would know that on this night Wilkinson stopped this kid for curfew violation and lurking in a strange neighborhood. Someday the information might come in handy on a criminal investigation.

An elderly lady, dressed in a bath robe, finally came out of the house. She crossed the street and told Wilkinson she was the boy's grandmother.

"He was over in the 2300 block of Penn," Wilkinson told her. "He's breaking curfew."

"What you doin' over on Penn this time of night!" the old lady screamed at the boy. "You go ahead and jack him up, officer, because when I get my hands on him I'm gonna jack his ass, too!"

She went back to her porch and watched as Wilkinson finished filling out the card, then gave back the boy's possessions. The boy walked across the street and into his house.

"She probably won't jack him up," Wilkinson said knowingly. "A lot of times they make a big scene in front of a cop, just to try to make you think that they are going to deal with it themselves. Most of the time they don't.

"You know, I had a lot of those F.I. cards on me when I was a kid," Wilkinson admitted. "I hate busting a kid for doing the same stuff I did. . . . After I became a cop, I went to see if they still had all the F.I. cards on me, but everyone of them was gone. Somebody cleaned them out for me."

* * *

It's now after 1:00 A.M. Wilkinson and Officer Reuben Chavira are on the way to pick up two Compton juveniles who are being held for auto theft by L.A.P.D. (Los Angeles Police Department) at an eastside precinct. Since two officers are needed for picking up prisoners, the beat sergeant doubled up Wilkinson and Chavira, but instructed them to hurry. He needed both of them back on patrol as soon as possible because things were really popping tonight.

The two officers are former partners. It wasn't clear whether their long-standing partnership was broken up by the salt-and-pepper directive (although since Chavira is Mexican, the team is actually integrated) or by the choice of the two men. Wilkinson admitted earlier that he and Chavira had almost come to blows on one of their last rides together.

"Reuben likes to come down hard on Title 6's—you know, the wetbacks," Wilkinson had told me. "You know, Reuben is Mexican himself, but being a cop has done something to his thinking—at least where wetbacks are concerned. This one time he really was hot to jack the turkeys up, but I couldn't see it. Jesus, Reuben got so hot he nearly turned on me. We almost had a fight right there."

Before leaving the station, Wilkinson and Chavira argued about who would drive. The sergeant had told them to take one of the new patrol cars, and get back in a hurry. That meant some fast driving in a nice car. Chavira got behind the wheel and wouldn't budge, even though Wilkinson argued stubbornly that driving was his job.

Finally, with Chavira driving, and nicely blowing the carbon out of the new carburetor, the two began discussing a recent shooting that had taken place.

For a minute or so I felt like I had come into a room during the tail end of a conversation, and I finally asked what it was they were discussing.

"Well, Bruce, it's a real bad story," Chavira said. "These two L.A.P.D. officers stopped a black guy one night—not far from here—and the officer who was approaching on the driver's side said the guy had gotten out of the car, then suddenly grabbed under the seat for something—like he was going for a gun. The cop shot and killed him. But then the cop couldn't find a gun. So he put a throw-away gun in the dead guy's hand. . . ."

"A what?" I asked.

Chavira looked at Wilkinson. "You see, some cops who are real fuckers carry extra guns just for this purpose. They file the registration numbers off, and just have them ready in case they kill someone who doesn't have a gun. Then they throw the gun down, and claim that it was the one the guy was pointing at them. That's a throw-away gun."

"Fuck," I said softly, almost unbelievingly.

"Sometimes it happens," Chavira said unapologetically. "In this case, the cop picked up this gun while investigating a burglary at a sporting goods store. The gun was just put down as one of the things missing . . . and the cop took it home and filed the numbers off, and kept it with him for a situation like this.

"The way I figure it, maybe the suspect did dive

under the seat like he was going for a gun," Chavira said, "and maybe it did call for a split-second decision. But any cop who carries a throw-away gun is looking for trouble. I mean, he's got to be a fucker to start with."

"What's going to happen to the cop?" I asked.

"It looks like they are going to try him for murder," Wilkinson said.

"Good," I said. "He deserves a murder one rap for that."

"Yeah," Chavira agreed. "I carry an extra gun. I mean, it's not a throw-away gun, because it's registered and everyone on the department knows I carry it. But it's a small gun that I hold in the palm of my hand, with my citation book covering it, when I'm sitting in the car writing out a ticket. That way, if anything happens, I won't have to go for my service revolver. You need all the insurance you can get on a job like this."

At the L.A.P.D. precinct—the same one, by the way which the cop/murderer was assigned to—Wilkinson and Chavira entered through the back door, and walked a few feet to the entrance of the jail. There was a large wooden box on the wall, with small separate lockers. They both took out their guns and locked them in the same locker. No guns allowed in the jail area. It doesn't take much imagination to figure out why.

Wilkinson gave the jail sergeant the paper work on the two juveniles, who reportedly were chased at speeds up to 100 mph by several L.A. P.D. units before they were apprehended in a hot car.

"I don't remember anybody by that name," the sergeant said. "When did they come in?"

"Look, I don't know," Wilkinson said, slightly

piqued. "Our sergeant just told us to come up here and pick up two turkeys that you were holding."

"Go see the lieutenant," the sergeant said.

Chavira went to talk to the lieutenant and Wilkinson and I waited by the gun lockers.

"Say, there's something I've been meaning to ask you," I said. "Why do you use the word turkey?"

"Oh, it's just slang," he explained. "Every department usually has its own word."

"But why turkey?"

Wilkinson laughed. "Well, because they're dumb birds."

Chavira called for us to follow him. A jailer led us to a small holding cell, and unlocked the door.

"Better watch it," he warned. "These guys are a couple of heavies."

Wilkinson and Chavira unsuspectingly entered the cell, and there sat two 12-year-old boys in red woolen caps. When they stood they were barely five feet tall.

"Jesus," I muttered. "These are car thieves?"

"You think we're kidding?" the jailer asked defensively.

"No," I retorted. "But I wish you were."

The jailer smiled narrowly and shrugged his shoulders.

An arrest following a street knifing.

In the still of the night, Sergeant Gary Taylor checks out signs of vandalism at a local elementary school.

2 A.M. The sergeant decided to keep Wilkinson and Chavira together for the rest of the night. He doesn't have two extra reserve officers to put with them in separate two-man cars. And two-man cars are a must in this city late at night. In fact, due to vacations and a schedule screw-up, there are only four cars patrolling the streets of

Compton tonight, when there should be twice that many. Wilkinson and Chavira don't like that one bit, because it means less backup for them in a time of need.

At a red light, both officers silently watched a young, strikingly beautiful black woman sitting behind the wheel of a car that was halted in the middle of the intersection. When the oncoming traffic cleared, she completed her left turn and drove past the patrol car, casting a longer-than-usual glance at the two young cops.

"You see that?" Chavira regaled. "She had Reuben written all over her lips."

"She may have had Reuben written all over her lips," Wilkinson said, "but she had John written all over her body."

Chavira cracked up. "Touché."

4

THE DEAD GIRL

"Until we can find time to solve this case, that guy is getting away with murder."

—Detective John Soisson, Investigative Division, Compton P.D.

The community of Watts borders on Compton's northern boundary. The Watts Towers, a monstrously large, strangely ornamental sculpture located in the middle of Watts, is viewed by some as a monument to black pride and by others as a mountain to a single black ego. Simon Rodia, an untrained architect, spent half a lifetime building the incredible structure.

Detectives Soisson and Barclay marveled at the work for the umpteenth time as they drove by it on Saturday morning. Two blocks from the Towers was the address they wanted. The people who lived there were close friends of the late Margaret Johnson. They had already been interviewed by other Compton detectives two or three times shortly after the murder, but in keeping with the new policy of assigning investigators on a day-to-day basis, neither Soisson nor Barclay were clear what information, if any, had been developed by the other investigators. They grumbled loudly that some reports were apparently never filed and others were only partially written, and suggested that certain homicide detectives on the department weren't worth their weight in cow turds.

"Every detective in homicide has worked this," Soisson complained. "One detective was sure the husband did it. When he checked out okay, the guy went after the dykes."

The two detectives' overtime work today was somewhat of a rarity in the fiscal-stricken department. But when Barclay told the captain about the new hot lead, he immediately okayed the expenditure.

The case had been sitting in the file open, or uncleared. Relatively little progress had been made since the shotgun trigger had been squeezed. When an immediate arrest wasn't possible (i.e., husband had an alibi; so did the known dykes), the case sat unattended. Periodically a detective brand-new to the case was given the assignment for the day. Once he familiarized himself with the case, the day was practically over. When he returned to work the following day he was given another fast-breaking assignment. Soisson was pissed about all this. He knew that if he could once again be freed of all his other duties (i.e., strong-arm robberies, assaults) and be able to concentrate solely on homicides and follow up on a daily basis the still unsolved cases such as this one, there would be a few less murderers walking the streets of Compton.

Then, homicide finally received the kind of ordained break it needed. A woman called and asked to speak to a homicide detective. Barclay took the call. "She told me she lived across the street from the Johnson woman. She said she had some important information about the case but was only calling us now because she had been scared. It seemed she was in her kitchen one afternoon a few days after the murder, with the window open, and heard these two guys. She peeked out the window and saw them leaning against her car in the driveway. She recognized them both. One was a young black who lived on the block, and the other was a young Mexican, also a neighbor.

The black guy was describing to the Mexican how he had killed the Johnson woman. The woman listened, secretly, almost unbelieving. Like everyone else in the neighborhood, she had of course heard about the killing. But it seemed incredible to her that the murderer would be leaning against her car, calmly describing how he executed the young woman. Then she became frightened. Very frightened. She decided not to call the police. What if the arrest didn't stick, and the guy came back after her? No, it would definitely be better if she didn't talk.

That was a few months ago. Now, when the woman called and talked to Barclay, she admitted that she had a difficult time sleeping; knowing what she knew about the cold-blooded murder. She wanted to tell him what she knew, but she definitely didn't want to go on the witness stand. Barclay was noncommittal about the witness stand—knowing full-well that the D.A. might have to subpoena her as a key witness—but he promised he would follow up other leads and try to get the same damaging information from other people. Privately, Barclay knew he would have to try to break the Mexican and get him to admit what his black friend had told him.

Barclay and Soisson went over the Margaret Johnson file. They saw that two other teams of detectives had interviewed the Watts Towers family, which knew the Johnson woman intimately, and were a storehouse of information about her friends, enemies, lovers, etc. The two detectives decided to start with them.

The house in Watts was a small, dreary-looking structure from the outside. It was situated in a community that would not encourage white visitors unless they carried guns and badges. The black residents were cognizant of the fact that any whites who showed up here were paid to do so. They were cops or car repossessors or bill collectors. No white person in his/her right mind would come into this neighborhood just to say hello.

Inside the house was even worse. Many of the walls were painted black, and there were different colored curtains nailed up on the windows. Two of the five rooms in the house were sparely furnished—the rest were empty. Six people—including the grandmother, mother, several children, and a boyfriend of the oldest girl—lived in the house. The floors were swept, and clean of garbage, and the detectives later pointed out to me that the cleanliness of the dark, little house was commendable for this neighborhood because many of the homes they must go into are ankle-deep in garbage. (Soisson told about the time that he went into a messy house in search of a suspect, and when he got on his knees and shined his flashlight under the bed a pair of pink eyes stared back at him. It was a huge rat. Another cop told about the time that he was helping to search a house and when he opened a dresser drawer he found a pile of dirty, used Kotexes which the woman of the house was saving for some reason. A family of young rats had comfortably made their nest in the pile of bloodied material. The smell was nearly unbearable.)

Soisson began the interview by asking the three persons present—the mother, daughter, and boyfriend—what they knew of Margaret's friends.

"Well, I know there was this one guy who she was really afraid of," the woman said. "He had shot her in the leg once before."

Soisson knew of the previous shooting incident, but he pressed the woman for more information.

"Margaret told me the way it happened," the 16-year-old daughter said. "This guy named Harry came over, and he was mad at her for something. He said he was going to shoot her and he took out a .22 gun. Margaret laughed and told him she was going into the kitchen to get a cup of coffee, and if he still wanted to shoot her when she came back, he could. That's the way she was. She was afraid, but she didn't want to show it. When she came out of the kitchen, he shot her in the leg."

"Yeah," the boyfriend interjected. "She called here and I drove over and took her to the hospital. The guy was gone when I got there, but she told me that a kid named Harry did it."

"You know how old this Harry is?" Soisson asked.

"He's about 16," the girl said.

"Did Margaret continue to see Harry after this incident?" Soisson said.

"Yeah, he dropped by a couple of times," the mother said, "but she didn't really like him coming by after that."

"She was afraid of him," the girl agreed.

"You know, she had to know the person who killed her," the woman said.

"What makes you say that?" Soisson asked.

"Well, she would never answer the door half-dressed," the woman said. "With just her bra and panties and short nightie on. She wasn't like that . . . unless she knew the person real good."

"How do you know she answered the door like that when she was killed?" Soisson asked.

"The detective who came here a few days after she was killed told me," the woman answered.

Soisson flinched slightly.

"Say, that's Tommy walking down the street," the woman suddenly said, pointing out the window. "He knew Margaret and also Joyce Jackson, who was a good friend of Margaret's, until they broke off a few weeks before she was killed. Joyce used to live with Tommy. You want to talk to him?"

"Yeah, call him in," Soisson said. Other detectives had previously talked to Joyce, who confirmed that she and Margaret had been lesbian lovers. Although Joyce did not appear to be implicated in the murder—at least not from the evidence at hand—there was always a possibility that further information about her relationship with Margaret might uncover something new.

Tommy was a middle-aged black man with gray hair and sloppy clothes. He came into the living room and sat down on the couch, across from the two detectives. (Upon entering the house, both detectives immediately went for seats that faced the front door, and placed their backs against windowless walls. This, they explained to me later, was standard operating procedure.)

After a few minutes of perfunctory remarks that pretty much repeated what the woman and her daughter had said earlier, Tommy offered: "I'll tell you, Joyce is involved in this somehow. She knows too much 'bout everything."

"What is it that she knows?" Barclay asked.

"Well," Tommy began, looking around at the other people in the room, "she told me that Margaret was shot with a sawed-off shotgun, somewhere around the face or neck, and that you could hardly recognize her afterwards. Is that right?"

"You have to understand that there are certain facts pertaining to the case that we can't divulge. There are certain things that only the murderer and we know about. And that's the way we have to keep it."

"Yeah, I know," said Tommy, shaking his head. "But the things Joyce knows. . . . She said this big green plant was draped over the body."

• • •

When the day was over, Soisson and Barclay sat in the detectives' bureau, a large neon-lit room with perhaps 20 metal desks. The room was deserted at this time of the weekend. They were methodically sifting, shifting through the stacks of paperwork on the case—as well as all the papers and other things that were found in the dead woman's house—as they discussed what they had developed.

"Can you imagine the information he gave out?" Soisson asked unbelievingly for the fifth time, referring to the Compton detective who had volunteered flowery details of the murder scene. "That kind of information should never be given out. That way when you hear it, it means something . . . because only the killer should know it. But everyone in town has been briefed on this case. That man should not be working homicide. That's all there is to it."

Soisson and Barclay had developed a series of damaging facts.

Fact 1: Neighbors reported that a young Mexican boy named Eddie, who lived a block over from the Johnson woman, owned a sawed-off shotgun. He used to fire it in his backyard, much to the discontent of the neighbors.

Fact 2: About the time the Johnson woman was murdered, the noise of the shotgun being fired in Eddie's backyard ceased. Eddie was no longer seen with the gun.

Fact 3: Eddie and the black teen-ager, Harry, were good friends.

Fact 4: Harry knew Margaret Johnson very well, and in fact, during some kind of argument, had shot her in the leg with a .22 pistol.

Fact 5: The police report on the .22 shooting quoted Margaret as saying that a car drove by her house and some unknown assailants shot her.

Fact 6: Margaret Johnson later admitted to detectives that she knew who shot her, but she was afraid to report him.

Fact 7: Friends of Margaret reported that she had told them it was Harry who shot her, and that she was afraid of what he might do to her.

Fact 8: A woman heard Eddie and Harry talking outside of her house, and the black youth said he just couldn't take the chance that the Johnson woman might press charges against him for the shooting.

Motive: Because Harry had a long criminal record, he couldn't take the chance that Margaret Johnson would testify against him and put him in jail for a long time. To keep her from testifying, he borrowed the shotgun from his friend and blew her up.

"The irony of it," said Soisson, "is that if she told us Harry had shot her the first time, he would be behind bars now. And she would probably be alive today."

Soisson and Barclay knew that the chance of finding the murder weapon was slim because it was probably buried somewhere by now. But they also knew that if they built a strong enough case, finding the weapon wouldn't be necessary for a conviction.

• • •

Six days after the Watts Towers interview, Soisson and Barclay were able to free themselves from other immediate crime investigations (the newer ones also take higher priority), and they picked up Eddie Sanchez for questioning. Soisson explained to me that at first the youth denied knowledge of the murder. "I told him I would put him on the hot box [lie detector]," Soisson said, "and he changed his mind and told us what he knew." The following is a partial transcript of that interview:

Interview is being conducted at the Compton Police Department, detectives' interview room, on 5 April

1974 at 1214 hours, with an Eddie Tim Sanchez. Subject Sanchez is MMJ [Mexican male juvenile], 16 years of age, DOB 8-7-57, 5-4, 130 lbs., light complexion, shoulder length long black hair.

Present in the interview room is Sanchez, Detective Soisson and Detective Barclay.

Q. Eddie, we asked you to come in today to ascertain whether you know anything about an incident which occurred in January on Elm Street, which is right around the corner from where you live. We have been interviewing several people in that area. Do you know anything about the shooting of this Margaret Johnson who lived on Elm ?

A. Yes, all I know is that he told me he shot her.

O. Who told you he shot her?

A. Harry.

Q. Harry who?

A. Harry Simpson . . . he is a Negro, he is pretty tall, I think he's about 5-foot something, he's tall, he light, he got kinda big eyes, he got a lot of bumps in his face.

Q. What were his exact words to the best that you can recall?

A. Well, he said, "Man I just shot that bitch." I said: 'Wow.'

Q. Did he say anything else?

A. He used a shotgun.

Q. Did he tell you what kind of shotgun?

A. A 12-gauge.

Q. Did you question him any further?

A. I didn't want it to go on, I was scared. I said, "Man, you just did a bad thing. . . ." I said, "They going to catch you, man." He didn't know she was dead.

Q. How do you know that he didn't know she was dead?

A. Because he told me. He said, "I wonder if she is dead." I said, "Man, if you shot her with a shotgun, she's got to be dead."

• • •

(I wrote the following section when I was about one-third of the way through my research. I have debated whether or not I should pull it out of my notes and use it. At the time I wasn't writing it for the book; I was writing it for myself because I needed to do so. I remember the intensity with which I wrote it as I sat in the sand near the surf line at Manhattan Beach one bright Sunday afternoon.)

Yesterday, 18 hours with the cops. Today is Sunday and I've made my escape to the beach. I had to get out of Compton for a while. I'm beginning to feel like a cop. Even driving here I checked things out like I would have if I was on patrol in Compton. What's happening to me?

Tomorrow will be another big day in Compton. Detectives are supposed to bust the killer of Margaret Johnson, the whore-Jesus-freak who was on her knees sucking on a 16-year-old's joint, begging for her life when he gave her both barrels of a sawed-off shotgun.

When her body was found four days later it was bloated, with skin slippage, and Margaret didn't smell good at all. Nothing worse than the smell of rotten meat. You can taste it. Smoke a cigar or sniff gasoline fumes from a car's gas tank, it doesn't do any good when you go back into a house with that kind of smell waiting for you. It's in your clothes, your eyes, your sinuses, your bloodstream.

Then there was the autopsy. Margaret's skull was sawed open, her face pulled back to her chin, her brains scooped out. A large Y-cut was made on her chest. All the organs were taken out. Life is gone. She is a piece of dissected meat. Margaret, open and hollow, now resembles a one-man canoe.

Two pretty, alive women are jogging by me now. Will their bodies ever be one-man canoes? Will they be manhandled by a county coroner as they lie on the table, before having their organs wrapped up in a plastic bag and thrown back into the fleshy canoe? Then to be honored in church, cried over, and finally ceremoniously buried.

Margaret, when she was found, was out of shape; her head a swollen watermelon with remnants of eyes and a mouth, decomposition having set in. But there was this young black guy—one of the more accomplished auto thieves in town—who got zapped by a rival gang member. (The guy Officer Jack McConnell was glad to see dead.) The pictures of his body were lifelike. The face was alive. The body was slim, muscular, athletic. In the center of his belly was a grotesque hole inflicted by a shotgun blast. When the coroner cut into the belly, the gut spilled forth—many feet of fleshy tubes falling out as if he had given a strange birth to a colony of large worms. If someone, somehow, could have shown him this picture when he was alive, would he have changed any? Would he? Could he? Or would he think this a proud combat death?

• • •

Although I have been writing this book more or less in sequence, as I am now writing this—the end of Chapter 4—I have already nearly completed the rest of the book.

Frankly, this homicide investigation has caused me some problems. Although I have been waiting for weeks, even months, for the Compton cops to solve this case, they have not been able to do so. It is not a matter of them not knowing who did it. They do know. It is not a matter of detectives Barclay and Soisson not wanting to clear this case. They do want to clear it very badly. Why, then, is a murderer walking the streets of Compton with the cops unable to bring him in? The answer may shock some of you, just as it shocked me. You see, the detectives are too bogged down with their daily routine to spend normal work hours on this now-aging case. And, unbelievably, ever since that one Saturday, they have been unable to get overtime approved by their departmental head, even though they are so very close.

So, as I am now feverishly approaching my final manuscript deadline, I have to close this chapter and the Margaret Johnson homicide investigation in this manner. It is not as exciting or as satisfying as having been able to follow the detectives as they put all the pieces together and arrested their man and interrogated him and filed a complaint with the district attorney. After all, this is the way it is done so entertainingly on television and film. But if not exciting, this story of one homicide investigation and the frustration of the overworked cops is honest, and painfully so. It seems that police work is not always entertaining or exciting or satisfying.

I had initially gone out on this case with Barclay and Soisson on one of my very first trips to Compton. Since then, every time I've gone back to ride patrol or hang around with the Narks or whatever, I've looked them up and asked what was new on the Margaret Johnson investigation. And each time they would tell me they hadn't been able to get to it because of their daily work load and because of the department's severe economic situation that made overtime almost impossible to get. "This is typical," Barclay admitted to me one afternoon two or three months ago. "So typical."

The next time I saw Chief Cochée I told him I was afraid that I would have to end the homicide investigation part of the book with this unsolved case rather than one of the solved ones, because as fate had it I had become involved with it. I told him the detectives seemed so close but were unable to get the time to finish it.

Cochée looked slightly perplexed. "Can't you end it by showing that we are ready to go out the door to make the arrest?" he asked earnestly.

"Well," I hesitated, "I guess I could." Maybe when I said that I was actually considering using a literary ploy to make an arrest seem imminent. But I have since thrown out any such temptation, because I'm simply not convinced that an arrest is imminent. Maybe I was a few months ago, but I'm not any longer.

Yesterday, I telephoned Soisson to ask my "anything new?" question again.

"No," he said disappointingly. "Nothing new since we last talked. I'd like to get some hours on this. But they are so tight on overtime. All this other stuff is going on around here during the day, and we just can't get to it. And until we do get around to it, that guy is getting away with murder."

Soisson said the policy on homicide investigations was the same: they were not assigned to one detective, but are scattered throughout the investigative division. In the meantime, each investigator has numerous other responsibilities. In Soisson's case, he is now responsible (on the investigative side) for all assaults, rapes, threats, disturbances, and shootings into residences. "What with our high crime rate, it's all I can do to keep up with my regular categories," he admitted. "The only way I have time to go out on a homicide investigation like this one is if my categories are low. But right now it's jumping around here, so there's no way that's going to happen."

I told Soisson my dilemma of ending this chapter on such a negative note.

"Can't you talk to the Chief and get him to give us some overtime?" Soisson asked. (Should a writer ask for that kind of special consideration when he is writing a journalistic account? I think not.)

"Well, I don't know. Tell me, what kind of case do you have against the guy right now?"

"Another neighbor of the dead girl called me a week or so ago and gave me some more information," said Soisson. "But the way it stands now, because there has been no gun recovery and no shells were found at the scene, we aren't going to have a ballistics match. So the guy is going to have to cop out or we're going to have to put him on a lie detector and break him down. If nothing else, at least we will know who did it, and he will be booked for the murder and it will go on his record."

Murder. I never realized how easy it could be to get away with.

5

THE COMPTON CONNECTION

"Oh, shit! We're the top narcotics unit in the country. We've pulled off more big deals than anyone."

—Sgt. Robert "Smoky" Stover, Narcotics Division, Compton P.D.

The self-proclaimed nickname of the Compton P.D. narcotics unit is "The Wild Bunch." The Narks prefer that to "The Mod Squad," a name used by the local press to describe this motley group of eight narcotics officers. Actually, a department the size of Compton's has no business with an eight-man narcotics unit. A unit this size would not have come into being if the city hadn't managed to pick up generous federal/state grant monies to pay for it some 2½ years ago. Before the grant, one lone detective worked narcotics in this city, albeit unsuccessfully.

The lone Nark's time was taken up mostly with routine report writing on every narcotics-related arrest made in the city. He initiated very few busts, turning over most of his leads and information to the big boys: the federal and state Narks. In those days, dope flourished on the streets of Compton. A person with money could literally buy anything on the streets within a matter of minutes. But now, with "The Wild Bunch" in town, the only street dope that can be bought is weed—and reportedly not very good weed at that.

After being in operation only a few months, and in that time effectively cleaning up the city's more onerous street-sales situation, "The Wild Bunch" quickly turned its attention to dope anywhere they could find it. They have since made big busts all over southern California: San Diego, Los Angeles, Palos Verdes, etc. They were even responsible for one of the largest marijuana busts in state history: four tons worth. This far-flung narcotics suppression activity is considered quite kosher everywhere. Once the out-of-towners give the local police the courtesy of letting them know they are working in their city, it's a wide-open ball game with no boundaries. They can set up stakeouts, arrange deals, initiate traps, and make arrests. When nonlocal Narks make a bust, the local police cooperate by filing the complaint in the local court jurisdiction—a procedure required by law. Persons snagged by "The Wild Bunch," usually late at night, are whisked off to the Compton jail. It must be a strange awakening for someone who has never even driven through this ghetto city to find himself herself sitting in this jail, of all places.

The Compton narcotics unit is led by a 27-year

veteran of the department, Sergeant Robert "Smoky" Stover. He is called Smoky because of the perennial pipe in his mouth, and the resultant bad smell that it fills the room with. ("I've never said anything to Smoky, but gawd! he must smoke shit in that thing," admits one Nark.) Behind his back, Stover is also called "The Digger," due to certain steps he takes to relieve himself of bothersome hemorrhoids. But on the department, friend and foe alike consider Stover one of the best detectives on the force—if not the best.

Not one to play down his own abilities, Stover says gallantly: "I have a weapon that is more dangerous than my gun. Ask anyone around here what it is."

One of the loyal Narks within earshot quickly answers his plea: "The telephone."

"That's right," Stover happily confirms. "The telephone. I can get a guy in jail without leaving my desk. It's just a knack I've always had. I keep after a guy and never give up. Eventually I get him. Always."

Stover is a small, slender white man, with drooping cheeks and jowls. His sport coat and pants seem to hang on his wiry frame. Somewhere underneath his coat is an incredibly large bulge caused by his pistol. It is seemingly the heftiest part of his thin body. But it would be a mistake to believe that the gun is a vital part of this cop. "The way I feel, unless some guy is threatening my life or somebody else's, there's no need to shoot him," says Stover. "I can always get on the phone and track him down. We can always get him another day. When I go after someone, I get him no matter where he goes."

Sergeant "Smoky" Stover, head of Compton's narcotics unit.

The Narks know they are oddball cops, and to a man they cherish the thought. With the exception of Stover, who never goes undercover to make buys anyway, none of them look, act, or talk like cops. None of them are easily visualized in a uniform sitting in a patrol car, although all of them have spent considerable time in patrol. No, these Compton cops are a different breed.

• • •

The pretty black woman, in her early twenties, is sitting at Stover's empty desk. Smoky is taking the evening off, a rarity, so the deal will be going down without him. Some of the Narks are relieved at the thought, much like any employee would enjoy getting away from his boss once in a while. The woman has a smooth, light-chocolate complexion, and her black hair is lying down flat on her head, in a tight, severe bun that meets in the back. A Nark is talking to her about a telephone call she will be making shortly. She does not appear overly happy about being here. She is a snitch.

Sandy was herself busted by "The Wild Bunch" for selling cocaine. It was not her first time, so in order to make things easier for herself—and possibly avoid state penitentiary time—she is working with the Narks. She will be setting up as many coke deals as she can, and each deal will be an ounce ($1000 worth) or better. She has good contacts, and because she is a woman, and pretty, the Narks believe she will be especially valuable. Most coke dealers will trust a woman before they will trust a man. And especially a pretty woman. They will often be focusing on the possibility of getting into her pants instead of feeling suspicious vibes. Also, being black is also an advantage because how many black women Narks do you know? Yes, the Narks are very happy about having Sandy working with them. They are planning to use her quite a bit, probably even more than she realizes. After all, what can she do? Refuse?

After Sandy makes her quick call, the seven assembled Narks get ready. They are wearing floppy hats, beards, headbands . . . everything that the best-dressed Nark wouldn't be caught without. Sandy has decided that one of the black Narks is the one she wants to take inside with her. She thinks he looks more like a guy she would be dating and using and selling coke with.

Officer Edward "Red" Mason has a handsome high-yellow complexion and his reddish hair is grown out in a large natural. He has a tough, unmerciful look, and fierce, piercing eyes. He is wearing a mid-thigh-length trench coat on his rather tall, medium-size frame. Before putting the coat on, he unstraps a shoulder holster that holds a large, mean-looking weapon. He puts his regular gun in a drawer, then clips a smaller automatic inside his belt. Meanwhile, one of the other Narks had snapped several Polaroid pictures of Sandy. ("We always take pictures of our snitches.") She looks at the camera, unsmiling. The Nark tells her to smile for one last effort, and she offers a tentative grin. That's the picture that goes into the files.

Red and Sandy will be traveling to the location of the buy in one of the several unobtrusive passenger cars owned by the narcotics unit. The rest of the Narks will be riding two to a car, three cars in all will be covering Red and Sandy. I'll be riding with Frank Brower and Percy Perrodin.

Brower, 22, is tall, white, muscular, and has long brown hair and a drooping moustache. He has been in narcotics for 2½ years, ever since the expanded team was formed. He is wearing jeans, a matching jean jacket, cowboy boots, and a wide-brimmed dope dealer hat. As he walks bowlegged down the hall to the parking lot, he looks like a handsome cross between "Hud" and "Easy Rider."

Perrodin, 27, a black, is smaller and stockier than Brower. He has a very black complexion, with large brown, smoky eyes, thick lips, and a medium-length natural. He is wearing baggy pants and a shirt that is hanging outside. Percy-has a natural, swinging walk that some corner brothers spend hours practicing. He talks in a rapid-fire "street" manner that is often punctuated with bursts of genuine laughter.

Also along for the ride is Jim, a friend of Frank's who has come along to see firsthand what his buddy does for a living. Since none of us have eaten yet, and it is already after 8 P.M., Frank stops at a McDonald's on the way out of Compton. While eh owing down on double cheese-burgers, Brower talks about something that is bothering him. "You're writing a book, huh? Frankly, I'm somewhat opposed to this type of public exposure. Like 'Police Story' did a show about Narks that was very real. Too real. I'm afraid that we might work a case for six months and then lose it when someone reads your book." Brower says the way he will deal with his reservation is simply by not talking about that which he considers too sensitive. I tell them that is acceptable to me.

On the way to the Los Angeles address where the drug deal will come down, Brower talks in generalities about what it's like to be a Nark. "We are able to deviate more from the rules than patrolmen or detectives. I don't mean doing anything illegal. It's just that we have more leeway. But we do have certain guidelines we have to follow, like the rules for entering a house. If we violate them, we are taking the chance of losing our case. Also, of course, no entrapment is allowed.

"As far as deals we make with snitches, there's only two things we can do. If we have just busted them, then we can go to the judge and ask that they be let out on their own recognizance. That is actually financial help, because they don't have to put up money for bail. When it comes to sentencing, we will go to the judge and ask that they get county jail time instead of state time. Also, we do some paying of informants, but not much because of our budget. The Feds go crazy with money. They give their snitches weekly fucking allotments. You know, $200 or $300 a week. They have paid as high as $5,000 for a case."

Brower estimated that about 30 % of the Compton Narks' time is spent on busts outside the city limits. "There are more users than sellers in Compton, and we want to go after the sellers. Most narcotics officers believe that a seller doesn't have to be operating in a certain city to affect that city's drug traffic. I think a lot of outside agencies are surprised at what we've been able to do in the last 2½ years. We're doing a lot of busts equal to what the Fed and State guys are doing. We didn't get the publicity on the 4-ton marijuana bust, but it was our informant who took us in there. The problem was collecting the money and manpower. We needed $110,000, so we had to bring in LASO (Los Angeles Sheriff's Office), and they ended up getting credit for it. The guy we busted was a big-time dealer from Mexico. He had fronted 10 tons on the street before we got to him. In joints, marijuana is worth about $200 a pound. So the four tons we got him with was worth about $1.6 million. The guy immediately posted his $100,000 bail, and then he actually showed up in court the first day to see what kind of case we had against him. After talking to his attorney, he decided to skip out on his bail and go back to Mexico. He's never been back since. But he's still a big-time operator.

"We've had a couple other really big busts, one involved 350,000 amphetamines and the other was 250,000 pills. Cocaine is where the real action is at now. Addiction to it is psychological rather than physical. Most everyone snorts. Coke is supposed to be a big sex trip. Speedballs are popular now. They are coke and heroin mixed together. The coke gives you a quick rush and heroin will keep it going for a while. The word is you feel overzealous and paranoid."

I asked Brower how Narks are able to convince dealers that they aren't cops when they can't snort the stuff. "Well, first of all, not everyone snorts it. Some people are just in it for the business. But if they do want you to snort, you just tell them you want to conduct business before pleasure. It's like a guy not wanting to get drunk before business. If they insist, you just tell them no and burn the case. You hate to do it, but you lose the case if you have to. After all, snorting drugs is illegal. Narcotics officers sure can't do it."

Tonight's deal, compliments of snitch Sandy, is for one ounce of cocaine. The agreed price is $1,000. Red is carrying the money mostly in small bills. Every single bill has been Xeroxed and the copies are being carried by one of the other officers. The deal is that Sandy has called this guy she knows who has contact with a big dealer. The guy's pad will be used for the transaction. She and Red are to go over to the place, and if everything checks out, the dude will call the dealer, who will either come to the house or designate another location for the deal. Neither Red nor Sandy are wired for sound, so the bust will come down when Red comes out of the house carrying his coat. That will be the sign that the dope and money have been exchanged.

"Half of a baby spoon of coke will get you high," Brower explains. "A baby spoon is about $25 worth. Coke is an expensive high. It's hard to have a coke party unless you're rich."

Brower said that he recently was involved in a $96,000

cocaine deal that fell through because the Compton Narks cannot put up front money for dope. "This dealer was smooth," Brower says admiringly. "We're sitting in his new Mercedes worth maybe $18,000, and he says we'll drive to within a block of where the stuff is. Then I'm supposed to give him $10,000 front money, and he'll go get a sample. If it's good, then I'm supposed to give him the rest of the money and he'll get all the shit. He says if he takes off with my $10,000, I've got his $18,000 Mercedes. What do you say to that? Really, that's a damn good deal. But we just can't put front money up . . . we not only can't afford it, but we can't take the chance. So I tell the guy that I don't even know if he owns the car. You know, it could be repossessed any time. He says he'll leave his old lady with me, too. And I say that she's no good to me because I don't know her. I mean, I don't even know if she's any good. So the deal fell through."

Not every police officer is capable of working narcotics, Brower contends. "Some guys just can't hack shuckin' and jivin' with some of these assholes. They can't get down and do the stuff with these kind of people."

We are now on the right street. Brower drives by the address, and there are several small cottages grouped in a semi-circle. The residence we are interested in is at the very back. Brower goes down the block, turns around and makes one more pass. Then he turns at the first corner, which is about four houses down from the cottage, and parks on the side street, with a view of the cottage. The other two Nark cars park in opposite locations around the cottage. All three cars are in radio communication; not on the regular police band, but on a special and private narcotics channel with no other radio traffic. This privacy leads to some interesting dialogue not heard on the regular police channel. On the ride here, Sidney Moore, 27, a 6-foot-5, 180-pound black beanstalk, who has only been in narcotics for three months, keys the mike on his Nark radio and puts it next to the car radio speaker that is turned to a loud soul station which happens to be playing his favorite record. Frank and Percy know immediately it's Sid's doing, and they crack up. "That Sid is a constant orgasm," offers Frank.

Red and Sandy pull up in front of the cottage and park. They get out and go to the cottage, knock on the door and disappear. Now the wait begins. There's no telling how long the deal will take to go down. Especially since the dealer isn't even here yet. It could be an hour, or five hours. It also depends on how well Red and the snitch perform, and whether the intermediary is overly suspicious. In fact, it's far from guaranteed that there will even be a deal made. It could fall through for any number of reasons.

"Most dealers don't like selling to strangers," Brower explains. "But like any businessman, they need new customers in case the old ones stop coming by. When you go into a house, you have to talk good and convince him you're not a cop. I always try to ask a bunch of questions myself, and try to keep him answering instead of asking me questions. You don't talk politics or anything like that. You just get down and jive with 'em."

An hour later, one of the Narks, John Garrett, leaves his car on the other side of the cottage and walks slowly down the street, with his hands in his pockets. When he reaches our car he bends down at the passenger window.

"Why don't you go and sit on someone's porch," B

rower says.

"I don't know," Garrett answers. "There are a lot of white folks around here."

Percy goes out to do some walking, too. Brower stretches out as best he can in the front seat, settling down for a long wait. "It's a motherfucker being a cop," he sighs. "You can put that in your book. Pussy waiting at home . . . a nice wife, and I can't go. Do you know police are number one in suicides by occupation, and second or third in divorces. I was a truck driver before I became a cop. Actually, compared to a lot of other jobs, this is a damn good job. For having only a high-school education the pay is damn good. And, you know, you might get your nut by writing a good story. We get ours by kicking a door down. I guess that's why there are brunettes and redheads."

An older woman has been observing our car suspiciously from a nearby apartment balcony. Brower turns around to look at her through the binoculars, and his elbow honks the horn.

"Goddamn," he says, putting the glasses down and turning away.

"It's nothing new for people to get suspicious of 'The Wild Bunch'," says Brower. "We went into a house one time and arrested a girl, then took her next door, where some of her associates were living. We kept them in there for 30 minutes while we searched the house. When we finally opened the door to leave, there were 15 LAPD officers all with shotguns surrounding the house. They all jacked rounds into their shotguns, and I slammed the door shut, yelling, 'Police! Police! Police!' I opened the door a crack and eased my badge out. They told us later that they had gotten a call that there was a kidnapping going on."

After two hours the Narks are getting antsy. "The Dodgers are on TV tonight," Brower says. "Red's probably in there watching the game."

"I'd be worried," Garrett admits, "if it was anybody other than Red. But I know he likes to talk."

I tell Brower I have to take a leak, and he says he'll find me a gas station. We only drive six blocks in search of a head when the radio cracks: "They're moving! The guy is coming out with Red and the girl. Looks like they're going for a ride. Yeah, they're getting in Red's car. Frank, can you pick 'em up if they go west?"

"Negative," Brower informs his colleague. "We're out of the area on a Code 100." (Code 100: An official toilet stop.)

"Forget it," I tell Brower. "I can hold it."

"Okay," Brower says as he reels the car around in a nifty U-turn. "We're approaching from the east," he says into the radio.

"They've pulled away from the curb," the radio voice continues. "Going west. John, can you pick 'em up? Wait, they are turning south. . . . They are going around the block, it looks like."

We are now driving in front of the cottage, and Brower pulls over to his previous parking spot to wait for further information.

"They're back on our street now. Going east, toward the house."

Everyone in our car ducks down out of sight.

"Looks like . . . yeah, they are parking again. We have a visual. Everyone else stay down. They are out, the old guy is really looking around. They are standing around out front. Okay, now they're starting back for the house."

"The old guy is suspicious," Brower says as he straightens up from his crouch. "I would be too if I was him. It's a suspicious business."

As the wait continues, Brower talks more about the "silly game" of narcotics busts. "All these search-and-seizure laws are too much," he says. "A cop has to identify himself from outside the door, and say he is here on a narcotics investigation. Then you have to wait a 'reasonable period of time.' Before you know it a toilet is flushing and all the dope is gone. Either that or you can bust down the door immediately, without introducing yourself, then get on the stand and perjure yourself in court, saying that you did identify yourself and that you did wait a reasonable time before kicking the door down. It's just a silly game."

Two cars pull out from a long driveway located between the cottages and a large apartment complex next door. Several people are in each car, and they quickly speed off. The Narks observe this, and there is some short chatter on the radio about it, but nobody goes after the two cars.

"How do you know Red isn't in one of those cars?" I say, asking the obvious question.

"He knows better," Brower says. "We can't follow everything. If he's crazy enough to get himself into a situation like that, fuck him. He'd be dead."

In a few minutes a new hopped-up Corvette pulls up in front of the cottages, and parks right in front of Red's car. A large, youthful black man dressed in a colorful shirt gets out and disappears among the cottages.

"He went inside," the radio says. "Must be our man. Either he brought the stuff with him or they are going for a ride."

"We'd better close in on him before he gets in that 'Vette or he's 'bye," says one Nark on the radio.

"I wonder how that hot car would run with square tires," Brower replies.

"Not a bad idea," someone says. "The only thing is, someone's got to get out there and square them without being spotted."

"Oh, let me, Frank, let me," Jim suddenly exclaims from the back seat. Jim has been bugging his friend all night to let him do something Nark-like. He said the whole operation favorably reminded him of Vietnam, where he spent several months in combat. "I could go out there and do it! No problem! Please, Frank." Jim, in his early twenties with a powerful physique and shoulder-length hair, could actually have passed for a Nark. In fact, when Frank introduced me to him as "an old friend of mine," I was suspicious that the guy was a fed or state Nark who didn't want to be identified. But that suspicion soon left as Jim continually opened his mouth and volunteered with childlike exuberance to play Nark. The guy was obviously enjoying himself so much that I secretly wished that Frank would let him go out and puncture the guy's tires. He'd probably do a helluva job of it, too.

"No, Jim," Brower says. "That's all right."

"Aw, Frank," Jim says dejectedly.

Brower laughs easily and turns around to look at his friend in the back seat. I wonder what Brower is thinking at that moment.

"Okay, the crook is leaving the pad," the radio says.

We see the big brother walking out to his Corvette, then matter-of-factly climbing in it. "Red's out. The deal's down ! Take him!"

Brower immediately starts the car and swings it around the corner, then hits the brakes hard and stops it sideways in the middle of the block, blocking- off the Corvette's exit. Two other Nark cars do the same from the other direction, and suddenly the street is filled with gun-toting longhair whites and militant-looking blacks. The guy sitting behind the wheel of the 'Vette doesn't move, even though he already has his engine running. He knows immediately it's hopeless. Two Narks order him out of the car, while pointing guns at him. He obeys, and soon is spread-eagled on the car, being searched for weapons.

Cars coming from both directions are halted by the action going on in the street. Several drivers gawk at the unreal scene, while others whip their cars around and head the opposite way, obviously not wanting to get in-volved in the middle of a shoot-out. Neighbors peer care-fully out of their windows, and some brave souls even venture cautiously out onto their porches. "Get inside, Martha," a nearby resident orders his wife. "It's the SLA!"

To protect their sources, two Narks slap hand-cuffs on Red and the girl. Meanwhile, five Narks and two observers storm the suspect cottage. Everyone has their guns out, and as we stay behind any cover that we can find, Brower goes up to the door and says, "Police! Open up!" A voice on the other side of the door says something, but the door stays closed. "Police!" Brower yells again. There is no sound on the other side. "Kick it down!" Brower suddenly orders as he and two Narks head for the door. They give it one mighty kick that splits the wood around the lock. Another kick literally breaks the door open, and the entire doorknob assembly falls on the ground. The cops immediately jump inside the house. As they run through a small living room, two Narks peel off for the kitchen and the rest head for the bedroom and bathroom. The bathroom door is kicked open and tall Sid yells, "Halt!" He is pointing his pistol at the back of a middle-aged black man who is halfway out the small window. The man keeps struggling to get out the window, and Sid and Paul Lane pull him back and wrestle him into the hallway. As the man falls to the floor so does Lane, who is hopelessly tangled in Sid's incredibly long legs.

"What the fuck you trying to do?" Sid yells at the man. "I almost blew your head off."

(The poor guy wouldn't have done any better if he had gotten outside, for a Nark and "Vietnam" Jim were waiting out in the backyard for him. At first the Nark had struggled with the picket fence, trying to get over it, but "Gung-ho" Jim smashed into the wooden fence with his feet and body and broke it down. His adrenaline was really flowing as he finally got a chance to participate. "It was just like fuckin' 'Nam," he told me later.)

Lane gets up, limping from hitting his shin on a small table. He goes into the kitchen and opens the refrigerator. Taking out a tray of ice cubes, he places one against his sore leg while the other Narks check the house for dope.

Red is carrying one ounce of coke, and the unfortunate dealer has the marked money. According to Red, the old guy in the cottage was left a small amount of coke for his efforts in setting up the deal. Although the bust will be good on the dealer, it won't hold on this guy unless they can find some shit in his pad. They search the house from top to bottom and come up with a couple of joints, and a plastic bag of suspicious-looking white substance that turns out to be diet sugar. While the Narks go through the man's closet and lift up his bed and overturn a bookcase, a small portable television next to the bed is flashing an unbelievable image. The fleshy jowls are familiar, but the mouth is moving strangely, soundlessly, in slow motion. Then it hits me. In the middle of a narcotics bust, President Dick Nixon is giving a State of the Watergate message. The volume is turned down, and somehow that seems entirely fitting.

In the living room, narcotics officer Paul Herpin is reciting "the rights" to the handcuffed man who is lying on his stomach in the middle of the floor. The Nark talks swiftly, then says, "Do you understand I have just read you your constipational rights?"

"Yes," the man answers hopelessly.

•　•　•

"Just wanted you to know we're going to be meeting somebody over in your city," Smoky Stover said into the telephone to the watch commander of the City of Bell Police Department. "Whether it's going to go down in your city is a horse of another color. We have to play it by ear. So if you hear about some black dudes with guns, you'll know what it's all about."

When Stover is off the phone, Herbin, a Latin-looking Frenchman, goes over the deal once more.

Through a snitch intermediary, Herbin has made telephone contact with a Mexican who will sell him a keg of white uppers, worth a couple thousand dollars.

"Okay, let me run this down again," Herbin says to the assembled Narks. "This guy is driving a blue Valiant, and I'm going to meet him at Ocean and Gage. Now, if he wants to see my money first, I'll go back to the trunk. If we are making the deal, I'll send Mrs. Stover back. That's the signal for a bust."

Mrs. Stover, a reserve officer, has been brought into the case by her husband because she speaks fluent Spanish. Judging from the heavy accent on the phone, Herbin isn't sure the guy knows enough English to conduct the deal. Bringing her along to converse with the dude in his native language will not only relax him, but will take Herbin off the hook. Although Herbin looks as Mexican as the day is long, he doesn't speak Spanish. Some of the Narks marvel at the ease with which Stover brings his wife into such deals. "I sure wouldn't involve my wife in this shit," says one Nark.

"I need a High Standard for this," Red says, heading for the armory to pick up one of the department's brand-new 12-gauge pump shotguns.

"He likes shotguns," Percy asserts. "They do something for him."

Commenting about the bust that came down two nights ago, Percy says the ounce of coke that Red bought was "damn good stuff." The black dealer is hurting, too, because he's already on probation for sales. That means he's facing a few years in the state penitentiary. The woman snitch worked out so well and did such a fine job inside that Percy is sure she will be used a lot more. "I'll tell you, women have been the downfall of many good men," he observes wryly. "That's why I try to fuck 'em every chance I get."

Today I'll be riding with Percy (driving) and Sid. We go in the back lot and get into the slightly souped-up civilian car and Percy drives it to the nearby gas pump. "Listen," he says to me after filling the tank, "you got to lean in that seat." I give it my best low-rider lean, and Percy smiles. "That's it."

Percy looks over at Stover's car, and the sergeant is getting his electronic listening receiver in place. A pretty teen-age girl is sitting on the passenger's side. "Hey, Smoke, is that your daughter?" Percy yells.

"No," Stover quickly lies.

"You been holding out on us. How old is she, Smoke?" Percy persists.

"Eight years old," Stover says, smiling widely.

"Shit," Percy says under his breath. On our way out of the lot, Stover is reaching up under his wife's blouse to make sure that the tiny microphone is in place. Percy leans out the window. "Can't you wait until you get home, Smoke?" he chides.

"Does Stover always bring his family along on deals?" I ask.

"No, it's the first time I've seen the girl," Percy says. "Listen, for your book, I want to be called Clark Dark. You know, like Clark Kent, only Clark Dark. That's me."

The car radio is turned up loud as we head for the freeway that will take us to Bell. Sidney is jumping up and down to the music. "What I want you to say in your book about me is that if I die, I die happy. 'Cause I'm doing what I like. That's my dialogue."

"Clark Dark" explains that 95% of the time, dealers are non-violent when they are busted. "They know we got 'em. Sometimes they try to run. We block them. Some of us shoot at them."

We are the first car at the designated intersection, and as we pass the blue Valiant we clearly see a Mexican behind the wheel, checking his rear-view mirror. Once through the intersection, Percy keys the walkie-talkie and, without lifting it off the seat, says: "Okay, the crook is waiting. We'll park north of the intersection. Watch it, he's definitely looking." (Unlike on television, an under-cover cop in this type of situation doesn't lift the radio mike to his lips. Even from a distance, such an obvious gesture would be easy for an experienced crook to notice.)

We park across the busy intersection at the back of a gas station lot. Herbin and Mrs. Stover have now pulled up behind the crook's car, and all three are out of their cars, talking. Stover, who is monitoring the conversation from two blocks away, says, "It looks like they're going to trip." (Trip: Travel some place else for the deal.) "Okay, they are going to drive to a public phone. Herbin is going to follow in his car."

We see the two cars pull away from the curb and turn eastbound at the intersection. Herbin is on the air now. "Looks like he doesn't have the stuff with him," he says. "He's got to make a phone call."

We follow several blocks behind, then when Herbin gives the location of where they have stopped, we circle around the location and park several blocks to the south. "We providing support," says Percy. "We the supporting cast. Some people like to be the stars, but I'm content to be the co-star. I don't even like to be the first one in a house. It might be the wrong house."

"The crook is making his phone call now," Stover reports over the radio. "Everybody hang loose."

"We busted this guy the other day who lived in a caged house," Percy relates. "I mean he had bars surrounding his entire house. The porch and everything. We knew he was dealing and had stuff in his house, but we knew we couldn't bust in and get to him before he flushed it. And he never seemed to leave the house. We sat on it for days. Then finally he came out to water his lawn, and we went after him. His wife was still behind the cage, a few feet from the house. When he saw us he yelled: 'Go do it! Do what I told you!' She headed back into the house. I pointed my gun at her and said: 'Freeze! I'll shoot!' She stopped. When we got inside we found two ounces of coke sitting right next to the toilet."

"The deal's not coming down now," Stover tells his men over the radio. "We're supposed to meet the guy back here at seven tonight. Everybody clear the area. You can take the mike out," he adds for the benefit of his wife. (The small mikes have a tendency to get warm, and when they do they can burn skin.)

"I'll get it out," Herbin volunteers.

"Go ahead," Smoky laughs, "if you think you can get away with it."

On the ride back to the station, Percy brings up the subject of his wife. "She used to really bug me about the long hours. One Friday night I got some potato chips and wine and took my wife along. I picked out this house that looked like no one would be coming home. And we sat there. I told her we were on stakeout. After about an hour and a half, she said, 'I'm tired. How long you going to sit here?' I said, 'As long as it takes.' About 30 minutes later I let her talk me into leaving. Ever since that day, I've been getting no more shit about my hours."

Percy's story delights Sidney. "You know what I told my wife? I said, 'Whenever you see me in a car with another woman, you don't know me.' She said, 'What?!' I said, 'Look, they're playing for real. My life is on the line.'" Percy roars with laughter.

• • •

Policemen today are concerned about two things, according to Smoky Stover. "When do they get off work and when is payday," he explains. "Fifteen years ago, a policeman did his job for the satisfaction of getting the job done. There was no such thing as overtime or compensatory time off. We weren't clock watchers in those days. We'd work through the night running down leads. In police work, a man's family has to take the backseat.

"Another thing; it's bullshit for policemen to take personal offense to supreme court decisions. Sure the courts have made it tougher for us, but I can still do my job. I just don't let the courts upset me."

Stover admits that he isn't sure whether the city will pick up the $230,000-a-year price tag on the present eight-man narcotics unit when the federal grant runs out in six months. Naturally, he would like to see the size of the unit remain intact. "Narcotics is big business," he states. "We are looking for supply lines. There is no dope in this town except for weed. They are so afraid of us. So we have to go out of town. But if you don't keep enforcement up, then the guys on the street aren't going to be worried about The Man."

Although Stover has worked and lived in Compton during its transition from a white middle-class town into an economically depressed black one, he doesn't blame the change in the residents' skin color for the high crime rate. "Twenty-seven years ago, Compton was a typical college town. Compton College was the first junior college in the state. It was well-known for football and track. The Compton Invitational Track Meet was one of the biggest around. In those days, the population was about 37,000, and we had 22 men on the police force."

Although the population has less than doubled since then, the size of the police department has increased six-fold. "Yeah, the department has increased," says Smoky, "but so has the business. When I first started, you might get only one call a month on the graveyard patrol shift. What did you do? Well, you rode around and shot the bull with anyone you could find.

"When the crime rate climbed here in the middle fifties, it did so nationwide. There was a depression in the Eisenhower reign, and a lot of people were hurting.

"The ethnic balance was bound to change here in Compton, because a large community of black people bordered us on the north and there were more blacks coming here all the time from the East and South. But the increased crime rate here wasn't the result of a changed ethnic makeup. The rate throughout the entire country went up and at the same time.

"I lived in the city until a few years ago. I own several homes here. What drove me off was the schools. My kids just weren't learning."

Stover is relating his story from behind his desk in

the narcotics office. He stops periodically to discuss a case with one of his men. . . . "No, parks aren't a good place to set up a meet. Parks are too hard to cover and they have too many people around." Or he stops while the black woman snitch makes a phone call, so that the person on the other end of the line won't hear any background noise other than the radio in the office that is playing soft soul music. Every time she makes a call, a Nark unscrews the speaker part of another office phone and listens; just in case his testimony is later needed in court. When Stover's attention is again directed back to our interview, he looks squarely at me and says in a no-nonsense tone: "All right. Continue."

After one such lull, I restart by asking: "How much does a snitch have to do for you in order to get special treatment?"

"If we busted a guy for dealing ounces, then he's got to go up to half-pounds. They've always got to go up the ladder for us. That's how we do it."

The snitch picks up the telephone again, so Stover stops talking. She dials the number, asks for her contact, then waits for him to come to the phone. Sidney, who has been giving Betty Shelby, the narcotic unit's secretary-receptionist, a bad time for the last 15 minutes, sits down in a nearby chair. Shelby, whom Sidney affectionately calls "Hot Mama," goes to the sink and fills a glass with water. She returns to where Sidney is sitting, and quickly pours the water down his neck. Percy, Sid, and "Hot Mama" all crack up, trying desperately to hold their laughs inside and keep quiet. Sidney, unable to control his laughter, leaves the room. Stover looks at the practical jokers but doesn't say anything. The snitch waits, and waits, and finally hangs up the phone. "I think the chick forgot to tell him he was wanted on the phone," she explains.

"Well, you can try to do that for us later, or maybe tomorrow," a Nark says, ushering the woman from the room.

"Okay," says Stover, "give us the rundown on the seven o'clock."

Herbin and Mrs. Stover begin their rundown. "We're supposed to meet the guy tonight and he's gonna take us to within a few blocks of where the stuff is," Herbin explains. "From what he said this afternoon, it sounds like a big warehouse operation. After we bust the guy, we'll get him to take us to the warehouse. When we meet him at seven, we'll all go to the location in our car." (Interestingly, there isn't any question in the minds of the Narks that, once busted, the guy will turn snitch. They all do. It's called survival.)

"Hey, Smoke, have the crook ride in his own car," Percy suggests. "That way Paul [Herbin] can give us directions over the radio if we get messed up."

"Sounds good," Stover says, puffing thoughtfully on his pipe.

The briefing breaks up and everyone begins getting ready to leave. "We need some more firepower for this," Red Mason says, getting the keys to the armory so that he can fetch his favorite weapon.

"You already got about 12 guns on you," chides Sidney.

Red says as he happily departs for the armory and the shotgun rack.

Once again I ride with Percy and Sidney. En route to the location, Percy spots a good-looking girl walking down the sidewalk. "Look at the ass on that woman," he enthuses.

"Well, turn the car around," Sidney says, checking the lady out.

"Too much traffic," Percy replies.

Herbin and Mrs. Stover meet the Mexican dope dealer, and he agrees to let them follow in their own car. As soon as he's back in his car, Herbin tells his comrades via the radio that they are going to a central Los Angeles destination, but first the guy has to stop at a gas station.

"Okay, the cat is out of his car, pumping gas," a Nark who is following Herbin and the crook reports over the radio a few minutes later. Then: "They're on their way. Heading east, toward the freeway."

All five Nark cars are rolling now, staying at varied distances behind the crook. In one car is Officer Dennis Ford, who is officially attached to a new special burglary unit. Riding with him is Reserve Don Messerle, who in an earlier chapter was riding patrol. Both Ford and Messerle have come along to provide added firepower in case the warehouse bust comes down. Messerle, who is a full-time county probation officer, puts in almost another 40 hours a week as a volunteer cop.

"Percy, where are you?" Stover suddenly queries.

"Right behind ya, Smoke."

"Good place."

To us in the car, Percy adds: "In my supporting role."

Once on the freeway, Stover is the closest Nark car behind Herbin and the crook. His car is also the only one with an extra antenna that is attached to the side of the car, in order to pick up the signal from the mike that Mrs. Stover is wearing under her blouse.

"Hey, Smoky," Herbin says on the radio. "That antenna is big as shit in the rear-view mirror. The crook is really looking, too."

"Okay," Stover says. At the next freeway exit Stover's car turns off. "Stay back," he tells his men. "As long as we've got contact with Herbin, we don't have to dog 'em."

The caravan continues west for 15 minutes, then Herbin notifies his cohorts that the crook is turning off at the next exit. "I've got to get off the radio in case he pulls over," Herbin adds. That means it's up to the Narks to keep a visual on the two cars without the help of Herbin's radioed directions.

"Okay, we have visual," Percy informs Stover, who has now caught up and is trailing the rest of the cars as inconspicuously as he can.

"Okay," Smoky answers.

We follow them for several blocks in the industrial area, and when they turn east on a cross street, Percy notices we are the only other moving' car visible on the deserted streets. "They're turning south on . . . looks like 9th Street," he radios. "Someone else is going to have to pick 'em up. We've been on them too long."

"We're four blocks south of you on 9th," says Ford. "We'll take them."

"All right," says Smoky. "Don't get burned."

When the Mexican and Herbin turn south we keep proceeding east. Two blocks later we turn south, too, and pull over next to a weed-infested field.

"They're turning east off of 9th onto . . . can't see the name of the street," someone reports. "Now north on 11th."

"Jesus, they're going to come right by us," Sidney

suddenly explodes. Just then the blue Valiant comes down the street, with only the deserted field between him and us. The Mexican guy is obviously looking at our car. He continues north, with Herbin following.

"Fuck," Sid says to Percy. "That's it for us."

A minute later Stover says: "Does anyone have visual now?" Nobody answers. "Let's find them," he says with slight desperation in his voice.

Percy turns the car around and goes north on 11th, and we go right by the cross street they are parked on. We drive by, and Percy and Sidney seemingly have their eyes straight ahead so as not to alert the crook.

"Smoke, we just passed them," Percy says. "They're at 11th and . . . well, two blocks up from Green, whatever street that is. All three of them are out of their cars."

"We've got visual," reports another Nark. "We're parking three blocks west of them. We can watch them from here."

"Okay, everyone else stay away," Stover cautions. "Let's don't flood the area with cars. For a while we weren't picking up anything, but we can hear a conversation now."

A few minutes later, Stover reports: "Sounds like the crook is going somewhere. Don't stay too close, but find out where he goes. Might be the warehouse."

Herbin shortly comes back on the air. "The crook just went for the stuff. He's headed north. We told him we hadn't eaten yet, so we're going to this restaurant on the corner and have dinner and wait there for him. Listen, he doesn't think he can get the pills tonight, but he says he can get some coke for us. We told him we were interested."

"It sounded on this end of the conversation like the

warehouse is nearby," Stover tells Herbin.

"Yeah, that's the impression we got," Herbin replies.

"We got him," another Nark radios. "Looks like he's stopping. We've got to keep going. . . . Okay, we went by. We don't have visual now. But it looked like he was stopping in front of a bar. Someone else better check it out."

"We'll take it, Smoke," radios Percy in his usual nonchalant voice.

Percy drives the four blocks to the small bar that appears so out of place in the block after block of truck yards and storage warehouses. We cruise by slowly, and Sidney sees the suspect's car in the parking lot across the street.

"The crook's car is parked across from the bar," Percy tells Stover. "We'll park in the next block and keep visual."

"Sounds good," Stover answers.

Percy finds an alley that is blocked on one side by a tall building and on the other side by a three-foot wall. By parking the car in the alley, we are able to look over the wall at the bar in the next block. There we sit for the better part of an hour. That could be the drug warehouse, but more than likely he is just using a phone in the bar to call someone in his organization, Percy explains. "I don't trust him," he adds. "He's likely to be carrying a piece."

Percy and Sidney discuss their boss. "Stover is the best detective in the department, but he's a slave driver," says Percy. "He do always get his man. He's not in the field that much, but he does miracles talking on the phone."

"Smoky is a bulldog," Sidney confirms.

"One time we got burned for $800," Percy relates. "Our guy made a mistake and handed over the money before he got the stuff. Then the crook took off. Smoky was pissed. We worked that case for two days, and we finally caught up with the guy. Nobody, but nobody, burns Smoky and gets away with city money."

Despite his respect for Stover, Percy admits he's tired of being a Nark. "We come in at noontime, Monday through Friday," he says. "If we worked a straight eight-hour day, we would get off at 8 o'clock. But that's not the way it works. We're out until midnight, one or two o'clock in the morning all the time. And we don't even get paid for overtime unless we make a bust. Like look what time it is now. It's almost 10 o'clock. If this doesn't come down tonight, we don't get paid for anything after 8 o'clock."

"Stover says that's one of the things wrong with today's cop," I offer. "That they are too worried about their paycheck and hours."

"Shit, man, I've got a family," Percy says. "For me, that comes before any job. Stover doesn't care if we never see our family. He brings his wife along a lot of times, so he doesn't have to go home to see her. . . . I figure we've already given about 20 hours to the city this week. No pay for them—just free time."

"So you guys want a bust to come down not so much for the typical cop reasons, but because you want to get paid for your time," I suggest.

"Yeah, well, it's nice when it comes down for that reason," says Percy. "Like the Tiffany bust. We got paid overtime for that." (The Tiffany bust was big news in the Los Angeles area and a real feather in the cap for the Compton Narks. Although I was in town when it was coming down, I, unluckily, wasn't riding with the Narks.)

Percy thinks for a moment, his eyes staring fixedly in the darkness toward the bar. "If this deal don't go, it don't go," he says philosophically. "Another will go. We can't get all the dope anyway. If we did, we wouldn't have a job. It's the same with crime."

"Here he comes," Sidney says, but before he can get on the radio Officer Ford, who is parked down the block on the other side of the bar, puts out the word. (Ford told me later that he had just returned to the car from being outside. He said he had wanted to get a closer look at the bar, so he crawled under a big truck parked near the bar, and watched. A few minutes later, a drunk staggered out of the bar and sidled up to the truck. He undid his zipper and began urinating, directing his stream underneath the truck. "He pissed all over me," Ford later complained. "God, I felt like shooting his dick off.")

"Everyone stay put," Stover orders. "We know-where he's going." A couple of minutes later, Stover adds: "We're picking up the conversation in the restaurant."

"You know, I'd much rather be inside dealing with the dealer than sitting out here waiting," Percy admits to me. "This is bullshit out here. I'd rather be inside, talking shit and getting a drink. Some guys let things drag out inside instead of getting down to business. Like this shit tonight. We're going to fuck around with this crook and get nothing out of it. I can just feel it. Inside, you've got to be mean and nasty. You've got to tell them to fuck off. I answer some questions, but not others. If they ask me where I'm from or where I cut my stuff, I tell them to get screwed. I don't ask them where they are from and how they do business."

"No deal tonight," Stover informs the Narks. "Apparently he couldn't get the stuff."

"See what I mean?" Percy says to me. "You win some

and you lose some."

"Wait a minute," Stover suddenly radios. "He is going to get us a sample of the coke. Herbin has to follow him to his house. They are leaving the restaurant now."

Once he is outside and in his own car, Herbin goes back on the air. "We're going east on the freeway to his house. Don't know how much of the conversation you picked up inside, Smoky, but he's going to get us a sample. He says it's real good coke. If we like it, he promises the deal will definitely come down tomorrow morning. Oh, something else. He claims his connection is an L.A.P.D. cop."

Percy and Sidney look at each other.

"Okay, when everyone takes off for the freeway, go in different directions," Stover instructs his men. His voice doesn't portray the excitement he is probably feeling about busting an operation that possibly has a crooked cop involved in it.

The Nark caravan is once again on the freeway following Herbin, who is following the dealer. It is difficult to follow one car's taillights in a sea of red taillights at nighttime on a Los Angeles freeway, so periodically Herbin taps his brake lights four quick times, and the flashing red lights can be seen for a good distance behind him. He also gives directions concerning the traffic. "Watch it, lane two is slowing up," he cautions. "Yeah, there's just been an accident in lane one. Stay out of one and two." The Nark cars quickly move over to lanes three and four.

"He's got his turn signal on," Herbin announces. "We're turning off at . . . the James Street exit."

The Percy-Sidney car is the nearest one to Herbin. "We got 'em, Smoke," says Percy.

"Now, south on the first street," Herbin says. "It . . . looks like Pine. I'm going off the air. He might be pulling over at any one of these houses."

Percy turns on Pine, and several hundred feet ahead the crook turns down another side street, with Herbin right on his tail.

"Go right on by," Sidney says. As Percy drives straight ahead, the two Narks look down the side street and see the two cars parked at the curb in front of the third or fourth house down the block.

"Did you get the name of the street?" asks Percy.

"No."

"We'll go by it again."

"Jesus, don't do that," Sidney protests. "He'll see us."

"No he won't," the experienced Nark says as he turns the car around. "He'll be too busy talking."

We pass the corner again. Percy decides not to park where they could look down the crook's street, because to do so they would have to sit under a bright street light. He parks a few houses away from the light.

"Smoky, they're out of the cars at the south end of State Street," Percy reports. "We don't need any more cars down here. Except somebody should cover the north end of State."

"We'll take that," Stover replies. "Everyone else stay clear. We're picking up the conversation. Sounds like the crook is going inside for the stuff while our people wait outside."

For Percy and Sidney it's nearing the end of a long night. Both of them have been working for about 12 hours. They have seemingly lost their interest in this case. It's obvious the bust isn't going to come down (they won't bust for samples . . . because samples are given, not sold). They would both like to wrap this business up as soon as possible and get home.

Percy is laying his head back on the seat as best he can, and his eyes are closed. Sidney, a nonstop gabber, continues his monologue.

"Goddamn," he says, trying to stretch out his giraffe legs, "now I remember what I hated about patrol. Sitting in the damn car all day. My legs are just not made for this." He opens his door and unwraps his legs outside—partially blocking the sidewalk. "Yeah, that's better. Now where was I? Oh, yeah. I was telling you 'bout that fat mama, Beverly. Good God, was she fat. I mean she wasn't just fat, she was fat fat! Must have been close to 300 pounds. But she was good to me. I'd go over to her house late at night, so no one would see my car in front of her house. . . ."

Percy is beginning to chuckle now.

". . . She baked pies and cakes and cookies for me. She could really bake. Man, I could see why she got so fat. I went over to her house two or three times a week for about a year. I was gettin' lots of other stuff, too, you know, real nice stuff. But Fat Beverly was always there any time I got horny. She loved it, too. God, she'd try so hard to move that big body of hers in bed. . . ."

Percy is much more attentive now. His eyes are open and he's looking at skinny Sidney as he cracks up at the story.

" One time we were really going at it, you know, I was on top of her really stroking away when all of a sudden I look down at the floor. Jesus, I didn't realize before how far off the ground I was. I mean, if I had fallen off that fat mama I would have broken my neck."

Percy is busting a gut now.

"Okay," Stover suddenly says over the radio. "Our people have the sample and are leaving. Everyone can Ten-19."

Percy, still in near hysterics, starts the car while Sidney, still talking about Fat Beverly, brings his legs in from outside and tucks them in as best he can.

Twenty minutes later the entire Compton Nark unit is in its office at the police station. Everyone is exhausted, but Stover insists on debriefing Herbin and his wife. They say the Mexican has promised the deal will come down for sure at 11 o'clock the next morning. The guy told them a lot about the operation. "It sounds very big," says Herbin. "This guy says he's on a weekly salary. They have everything, supposedly all good stuff." (A fast chemical test on the sample of pink coke the guy gave Herbin shows it's very good quality.) "He says there are a couple of doctors involved in the operation, and also an L.A.P.D. cop. Now just how much of this story is true, I don't know . . ."

Midway through the briefing, Stover looks scoldingly at Percy, who is sitting in the far corner with his head down on a desk. "You with us, Percy," he says firmly. "Right," Percy responds wearily, not raising his tired head.

• • •

The next day is Saturday, and the Narks are gathering in their office at 10 A.M. They usually don't work weekends because of all the extra hours they work on weekdays, but no such luck today. Herbin makes his phone call but he can't get a hold of the Mexican dope dealer. Since everyone is here, they might as well try to get some deal going, Stover suggests.

Red telephones Sandy, and she says she is willing to try to set something up for them today. She doesn't have a car, though, so somebody will have to go pick her up at her beach community apartment 30 miles away. Red and Percy volunteer, and I ride along with them.

I ask Percy, who is driving, how much danger Sandy the Snitch is really in. We heard that the black coke dealer who was busted a few nights ago was already out on bail, and that he was trying to find the girl. He apparently went to her parents' house (where she hasn't lived for years), and they told him the cover story: she's in jail, unable to make bail.

"She's in danger to a certain extent," Percy admits. "But I doubt anybody would try anything. One informant did 100 deals for us. She might do that many. It's easy for her. All she has to do is walk into a club and some dude will get on her."

"If she scores today, she'll make 50 bucks," Red says. "That's a little extra incentive. A snitch is most valuable to us if she is willing to testify. She is not afraid to do that. In other words, she can go in and buy the dope and all we have to do is write the report. We don't have to buy the dope ourselves."

Sandy's apartment is a magnificently decorated pad in a high rent district near the ocean. She has two hard-to-find antique telephones (which do work), an expensive color television and stereo, a staggering record collection, closets full of clothes (I excused myself to go to the bathroom, then silently checked out her bedroom, which is complete with ceiling mirrors), and much, much more. How does she afford these things? Not because she's a hard-working girl in the best Protestant-work-ethic tradition. Rather, she is a user of people. She has cunningly, selfishly, efficiently used people all her adult life, she admitted to us somewhat proudly while we sat in her living room watching her make several phone calls in an effort to set up a dope deal. Percy is sipping wine, staring at her wordlessly from across the room. Red, sitting near her, is more open and talkative and he appears to be flirting with her, which she happily takes notice of.

It was only natural and in character for Sandy to become a willing and even eager snitch after she was busted because it was to her obvious benefit to do so— namely, by staying out of jail. There is little apparent remorse for setting up deals with drug acquaintances so that the Narks can bust them. Although she was an accepted member in good standing in the drug community just weeks ago, she has now switched sides. For how long? Only until it benefits her no longer. And this the Narks are very aware of.

"Not long ago I flew to Georgia on a coke delivery," she tells us. "The coke was in a baby powder can. They were going to give me some coke and a few hundred dollars for the delivery, but on the plane I got to thinking about all that coke. I was going to try to take off with it, but when I got off the plane at Atlanta these two guys were waiting for me. They had guns, too. I gave them the can."

Sandy is now making her sixth phone call in an effort to track down a certain big dealer that the Narks would just love to bust. (Red: "If you can get him, you'll get some real bread. The Feds have been trying to bust his ass for some time." Sandy: "Yeah, he knows the Feds want him. He's always bragging about how strong his operation is and how he's got a plane and a fast boat and how nobody is going to catch him. He's into coke, heroin, everything.") She has two personal telephone number directories that are filled with drug-connection phone numbers. The guy isn't at this number either, and it's the last one she has for him.

"Do you know anyone else you might be able to get some stuff from today?" charming Red asks.

"There's this girl over in Manhattan Beach," Sandy says. "She's kind of after me, if you know what I mean. I saw her at a party a month or so ago, and she said anytime I needed something, give her a call."

She makes her phone call. When the girl answers, Sandy is slick. She gets right to the point: "There's this guy I've been messing with for a month. He's got money and he's a sucker. I've talked him into buying an ounce. Can you? Good. Sure, I'll call you back in an hour. Oh, listen, how much? $1100? That's okay. I'll call you later."

The Narks tell her we'd better head for the station, and she can make her call from there. "Yeah," she says, "my boyfriend . . . my main man, gets off from work in 30 minutes. Sometimes he stops by here. He doesn't know anything about what I'm doing. He thinks I've been going straight for a long time."

"Is he big?" Percy asks seriously.

"Yeah, real big," she answers. "Makes me look like a dwarf."

"We better get going," Percy says.

"Yeah, we'd have some explaining to do if he popped

by while we were here," Red remarks.

"Oh, Lord, would we!" Sandy says, her eyes going wide. "Just let me change real fast, and I'll be ready." Within a few minutes she has changed from a fashionable pants suit to a slinky miniskirt.

In the car, Red, who is sitting on the passenger's side, continues to jive with Sandy. She and I are in the backseat, while Percy is driving. Sandy is getting a kick out of the talkative Nark.

"There is a difference in white women versus black women," Red continues. "A man got to be aggressive with black women, or they run you over."

"That's right," Sandy confirms, smiling widely.

"From what you have told me, it sounds like you are messing around with lots of guys," Red says, peering at Sandy over the top of his dark glasses.

"Oh, yeah, I've always been that way," she says.

"I take it you don't love your boyfriend. The big guy."

"I just care for my old man," she answers.

"I had an old dog for six years and when I had to kill it, I practically died," explains Red. "And like I've got this old '66 VW that I don't want to get rid of 'cause I've had it so long. That's how you feel about him."

"Yeah, that's right," she says again. Suddenly turning toward me, she says: "Listen, don't put my address in your book. I don't want him to know anything about this business." (Sandy is not her real name.)

While Percy silently drives, Sandy and Red continue their rap session. "Black men just want to be the best lovers," she says.

"It's an ego trip," Red agrees. "Now me, I've gotten over that. This shit about 'is it good' or 'are we going together' don't mean nothin' to me anymore. Hell, I'm coming off with or without you. You understand where I'm coming from," he adds, looking into the backseat and once again peering over the tops of his shades.

Sandy is cracking up like mad, and Red continues, lest he lose his timing.

"The main thing in life is me. Everyone should think that way. You might feel sorry for a guy with a one-inch pecker, because you'll wonder who is he possibly going to satisfy? I'll tell you who: himself. For me there's no more of this looking pretty. I'm just going to hit it as hard as I can and as long as I can, and when the clock strikes nine if you don't have yours, I have mine."

Sandy is ready to split a gut now, and even Percy is cracking up at his partner. "I knew . . . you were cold," she says between laughs. "But . . . shit. . . ."

A few minutes later, Sandy directs the conversation to the subject of Sidney. "I really like him," she admits. "I was suspicious of him that time. When he blew the coke, he blew out, not in. And he did that twice. But I went ahead and made the deal with him anyway. Then when we got outside Sid said: 'Don't want to upset you but you're under arrest.'"

"Why do you like him so much?" Red whines, pretending to be jealous.

Sandy smiles at that thought. "He says things that make me feel good. Like he told me he put his best friend in jail for dealing. That makes me feel better."

"Shit, I'd put my mother in jail for dealing," says Red.

"Not me," Percy interjects. "Hell, I never would do that."

"Would you rather have two white cops go over and

bust her?" Red asks.

"No, I wouldn't," answers Percy. "If it came down to that, I'd have you do it."

Sandy is now singing in a high, monotone voice to the loud music coming from the car radio. "You make me feel so brand-new. God bless me with you. I sing this song for you. You make me feel so brand-new."

As the car pulls into the police station lot, Sandy, looking at the assembled Porsches and Corvettes in the employees' parking area, says forlornly: "I want a sports car for the summer."

"Sandy," Red says, again peering over his shades, "you do enough work for us and you can. Believe me."

• • •

Sandy tries her telephone call but there is no answer. "It's been almost an hour and a half," she says, shrugging her shoulders.

While everyone waits, some hoping for a deal to come down, and others hoping that everything will fall through quickly so that they can still salvage this beautiful Saturday, it becomes storytelling time.

"I was at this one party in Beverly Hills," says Sandy, "and a whole bunch of Hollywood people were there. They are really into coke. I took an ounce home with me afterwards . . . it was just leftovers. At another big party I was at, a couple of Narks snorted $200 worth of coke before they made the bust. Goddamn!"

"Have you ever heard of pink coke?" Smoky suddenly asks.

"Pink?" Sandy hesitates. "Wait . . . yeah, there was

suppose to be some around a year or so ago. Think it was from Mexico. Heard it was powerful stuff."

"Oh, yeah, it's powerful stuff," Smoky says, taking a deep draw from his pipe. "We ran into some the other night. I was just wondering if you ever heard of it."

"I remember some guy was trying to set up some kind of a Hawaiian connection with the pink stuff," Sandy volunteers.

"Did I ever tell you 'bout Hawaii?" says Percy to no one in particular. "This was years ago . . . I was standing around on Hotel Street and this patrol car rolls up with two cops in it. One guy rolled down his window and said if I wasn't gone in three minutes, he would kick my ass. In three minutes he was back, and I was still standing there, and those two big cops got out and kicked my ass. . . . They don't like niggers in Hawaii."

Smoky laughed as hard as anyone at Percy's tale. Percy looked at his superior. "Hey, Smoke, how come you been holding out on me 'bout your daughter," he chides. "Goddamn she's nice looking."

Smoky hides his face in a cloud of smoke.

"I'm tellin' you, Smoke, that's such nice stuff a brother is just bound to come a-callin' one of these days," Percy continues, while the others in the office begin soft giggling. "Hey, Smoky. Guess who's coming to dinner!" Percy breaks up, joined by everyone—including Smoky.

"Okay," Smoky says, trying to reestablish a business-like appearance. "Sandy, try your phone number again."

She does, and there's still no one home. "She is probably at work by now. I think she starts work at two o'clock."

"Where does she work?" Smoky asks.

"She drives a taxicab."

"You know where?"

"Santa Monica," Sandy replies.

"What company?"

"I've got her card in my wallet," she says, reaching into her purse. "Yeah, it's Green and White Cab."

"Try to reach her through the dispatcher," Smoky orders.

"I'll try, but I don't think they do that," says Sandy as she reaches for the phone. "Hello. . . . Can I get in touch with Sheri Carter? . . . Oh, she's out. . . . When do you expect her back? . . . Not till then? . . . Thank you, good-bye."

Sandy explains: "No, they can't reach her for me. She's out until she gets off at eight o'clock. But what I can do though is get in town and call for her taxi."

"Let's do that," Smoky says, anxious to get the show on the road.

Smoky gets out the marked money and asks who is going in with Sandy. "I am," says Percy. (Earlier in the afternoon, Sandy had selected Red. But then she changed her mind. She said Percy looked more like a sucker than Red.)

"Okay, you take your car," Smoky says, knowing that Percy's yellow Corvette would look more natural than one of the Nark cars. "You guys try for two ounces."

Stover reaches into his drawer and pulls out the marked money—mostly 20-dollar bills. He counts out $2400, then has Red double check the count. It's right on the money.

I'm riding on this trip with the Latin-looking Frenchman: Paul Herbin. I'll be riding shotgun this time.

Not that I'll be holding a shotgun, but I'll be in the passenger's seat. A car with two guys in it looks less suspicious than one with three dudes. Herbin lays the shotgun on the floorboard, the barrel resting inches from my feet. Everyone else is getting into cars in the lot. The Corvette pulls up next to us and to our surprise we see Sidney behind the steering wheel, with Sandy next to him.

"Hey, why the switch?" Herbin asks Red, who is walking toward his car.

"Don't ask me," replies Red.

"I think Sidney is attracted to that young lady," I say to Herbin.

"Yeah, Sid is playing games," Herbin says under his breath.

Everyone leaves the lot at about the same time. Sidney is leading the pack in the Corvette, but there is no close following of each other because we all know where Sidney is headed.

A couple miles east of the police station, Herbin approaches a red light and stops behind a long line of cars. Directly to our right is another car stopped, with a black man behind the wheel and a white woman with long light-brown hair sitting on the passenger's side. Herbin stares hard into the car, while the man and woman keep their eyes fixed straight ahead.

"I always check out a white chick with a black dude," he admits. "It might be Patty Hearst. I think eventually she'll show up in this town. The shoot-out wasn't that faraway, and it was in the same type of community as Compton. And anyway, any major crime that occurs and has black people involved, the wanted always end up in Compton."

I don't know if it was auto suggestion, but when I took a longer look at the pretty white woman in the next car she did indeed look like Patty Hearst. Then she turned her head toward the black man, and smiled. The wide smile very much resembled the photo I had seen so many times of Patty Hearst. (The high school graduation-type photo with her smiling innocently at the camera, with her pretty long hair resting on her shoulders.)

As the light changes and the traffic starts moving, our lane is slowly moving. The suspect car is really moving in the right lane, and it makes several quick lane changes.

"They're sure in a hurry," says Herbin as he tries to catch them. He sees Red's car in traffic ahead. Red and the suspect car catch the same red light, and we pull up several cars behind them.

Herbin picks up his radio mike. "Hey, Red, is that P.H. in the brown car next to you? She smiles like her."

Red, who must have other things on his mind, doesn't answer. We pull ahead of Red when the light changes, and as Herbin moves in and out of traffic he can't close the distance between us and the suspect car. "Where are the patrol units when you need one?" he says in frustration as we approach the Harbor Freeway under-pass. "I've been looking for one ever since I saw them. I'd radio them to pull this car over and check it out."

The brown car whips onto the north entrance of the Harbor, and we continue under the freeway, heading due west for the beach. "Oh, well, I got the license number," he says. "We can check it out when we get back."

Sidney gets lost several times on the way to the beach, and Herbin is cursing that Percy should have driven the 'Vette. "He knows his way around," he complains. "Sidney doesn't."

Finally, the entire Nark caravan pulls in a Safeway parking lot in Santa Monica. A green and white cab pulls up in front of the store, and Stover says on the radio: "Is that her?"

"Negative," Sidney answers. "That's a male driving."

"Looks like a female to me," Stover insists.

"Not with a moustache he don't," Red says.

Smoky comes back with: "You never know these days."

Sandy goes with Nark John Garrett to make a phone call from the store. She is going to try to have the lesbian-dealer's cab dispatched to this location.

Percy is pissed off. He didn't like the last-minute switch with Sidney, he didn't like the way the deal was coming down, and he didn't like the waste of his Saturday. He knew if the deal didn't come down—which he correctly suspected would be the case—that he was giving this fine afternoon to the City of Compton, free, gratis.

"Kiss my motherfucking black ass, right in the crack," Percy says bitterly to no one in particular. "If this deal doesn't come down, I'm getting into my car and splitting. Right now!"

Stover has ordered everyone back to their own cars so the Nark mob scene doesn't attract undue attention. Red leans inconspicuously against our car.

"Say, Red," I say. "Back there a couple of hours ago, when we picked Sandy up, you were really rapping with her. How much of that was an act?"

"I know what that bitch is all about," Red says, staring into my eyes with a strange intensity. "I grew up in Compton. I've seen these kind ever since I can remember. She was facing three years for the bust we got on her. So she'll be a good snitch for us, as long as we keep a foot at her head. If she got the chance, she would rip off that $2400 Sidney has in his pocket. I know that for a fact."

Sandy the Snitch came back from her phone call. The girl had taken off early from work. The deal was off for today.

Percy immediately ordered Sidney to get out of his car, and he quickly slipped behind the wheel of his souped-up 'Vette and took off. He was the only Nark who wouldn't have to go back to the police station to drop off a city car. And Red would have to drop Sandy off at her apartment 30 miles away before he could even do that.

Yes, this afternoon narcotics officer Percy Perrodin was lucky. He had a nice head start on the other Narks as far as trying to salvage this Saturday afternoon.

6

SURVIVAL

"I spent a year in an open fire zone in Vietnam without getting a scratch. Then I became a Compton policeman and got shot."

—Patrolman Raymond Maillett, Compton P.D.

Twenty-four-year-old Raymond Maillett, a handsome, dark-haired, olive-complexed man with a trim, agile build, has been a Compton policeman ever since he turned 21. He is married, with no children.

Compton, when it was a white, moderately affluent suburb, was Millett's home town. He went to school here, then enlisted for a two-year hitch in the United States Marine Corps. Following his discharge, he came back to Compton and took a routine field services job with the city. When an opening occurred in the police department, Maillett quickly applied and tested for it and was appointed to the position. He has since moved out of Compton. His parents have also fled from Compton in the continuing exodus of the few white families left in the city.

While in the Marines, Maillett spent 13 months in an open fire zone in Vietnam. There was none of the usual Marine spit-and-polish in his unit because they were too busy trying to stay alive. "We'd go three and four months without a bath," Maillett recalled. "Once in a while we'd find a stream and if we had time we'd try to scrub up. The worst part was the jungle rot. Some guys were just covered with it. Big scabs on their arms and legs. It looked bad and felt a lot worse."

Maillett was assigned to a small, select, 15-man unit which usually operated on its own. When there were rumors of Viet Cong in a village, this unit would respond. If they found "Charlie," they would clear them out anyway they could. The unit had a 50% casualty rate. Since Maillett was the smallest man in the unit, he was the official Tunnel Rat.

"When we thought someone was hiding in a tunnel, it was my job to crawl in and take a look," explained Maillett. "One time I got into a fire fight in a tunnel. Are you ready for that?! I used my .45 pistol and killed a guy down there. He had the advantage, too, because I was il-luminated by my light."

Maillett went through 13 months of combat in Vietnam unscathed. Then, a year and a half ago, he was shot by a sniper on the streets of Compton, becoming only the second Compton policeman ever shot. (The other incident occurred five years ago. An off-duty officer was riding a motorcycle when he was shot in the neck.

He survived and is now an F.B.I. agent.)

"It was a night traffic stop and I was the backup officer in a two-man unit," explained Maillett. "Everything seemed to be all right. I was standing on the sidewalk, midway between the patrol unit and the other guy's car. My partner was writing a ticket on the hood of our car, using the car's spotlight to illuminate his book."

The bullet came in at a 90-degree angle from the direction that Maillett was facing. It came in from the right, on a flat trajectory, parallel and less than an inch away from his stomach. It hit him in the left forearm and the bullet lodged in the muscle and bone near his elbow.

"A few seconds after the shot a car that was parked right across the street sped away," Maillett said. "There were two guys in the car and we just knew it had to be them. The other officer pulled his gun, and I drew mine. We were taking aim on the car, and would have squeezed off some shots, except that a patrol unit coming toward us had heard the shot and spotted this car, so they drove over the island and took off in pursuit. The unit was right in our line of fire.

"It's a good thing that happened because those guys in the car didn't do the shooting. The sniper fired from a house on the corner, we found out later. If it hadn't been for the distraction of that car, we might have gotten the guy. It took the backup unit about a half-mile to stop the suspected car. When the officers got out, they were so mad they pulled the guys out through the open windows. You have to remember, though, at the time they were prime suspects in a cop shooting."

Maillett said the shooting, which caused him to be off work for six months, has made him more observant of things going on around him. "I always thought that if anything was going to happen, it would be from the guy we had stopped and were talking to. But now I look all around. I try to be aware of what's going on across the street and in the cars that drive by. . . . During those six months that I was off, I spent a lot of time on the beach, just resting and thinking. I thought a lot about my job and myself and my future. It did seem ironic that I went through the war without anything happening, and then for it to happen now. But I never thought once about quitting the force. The odds are with me. No Compton officer has ever been killed in combat. And I was only the second Compton officer to be shot. And there are 138 men on this department. So, next time it happens, it'll be someone else."

Maillett is convinced the bullet was not meant for him personally. But he said there are two other distinct possibilities. "My partner is not well-liked on the street. Everyone knows it. If it was meant for anyone, it was probably meant for him. Either that or it was meant for anyone wearing a uniform and badge." (Maillett's partner that night was Officer Robert Quintana, a volatile Latin who is viewed with mixed emotions by his fellow officers. Ever since the shooting incident, Quintana has worn a $55 bulletproof vest under his uniform.)

Patrolman Robert Quintana's bulletproof vest. Chicken? No way. "If I was chicken, I wouldn't be a cop."

Maillett's partner tonight was Ernie Booker, 25, a rookie cop still in the 28-week police academy operated by the Los Angeles County Sheriff's Department. Booker, who is married and is the father of a five-year-old boy, was anxiously looking forward to graduating in a few weeks. He said what he was learning in the classroom was fine, but he knew that "reality" was to be found on the street.

On patrol, Booker was behind the wheel and Maillett was the passenger officer. Early in the shift they simultaneously spotted a red Cadillac run a red light. Booker flipped on the rotating red light and took off after the car. (Normally, traffic citations are rather rare in this city. In 140 hours of riding patrol, I saw only four citations issued. It seems that the police cars are usually too busy responding to major calls to worry about relatively minor traffic violations. Also, I'm sure, because there are so many heavy crimes coming down here the cops don't need the diversion of harassing motorists, like so many bored suburban cops do in peace-loving communities.)

When the Cadillac pulled over, Booker stopped the unit directly behind it. As he got out and cautiously approached the car, Maillett opened his door and stood behind it, with the radio's microphone in his left hand and his right hand resting on the stock of his holstered gun. Maillett gave radio communications the car's license number, and within seconds they would know whether the vehicle had any wants or warrants out for it. (In other words, whether the vehicle was stolen or had been used in the commission of a crime.) When Booker reached the car, the driver opened his door and stepped out. He followed Booker back to the hood of the patrol car, where the officer began writing out a ticket. The driver, a young black man, stood casually between the two officers. Maillett alertly kept his eye on the driver, the woman passenger still sitting in the car and the normal street activity going on around him.

When Booker handed the man the ticket for his signature, he noticed that the guy's pants zipper was down. "Sir, you'd better zip up," Booker said politely.

"Oh, shit," the embarrassed man said as he pulled up his zipper. He laughed good-naturedly and added: "You'll probably give me a ticket for that, too."

When the two officers were back in the unit, Maillett began a critique of Booker's handling of the stop. "There are two things I want to say," Maillett said. "First, remember to always stay as close to the car as you can, Second, never go past the post behind the driver. Make him crane his neck to see you. That way, if he's going to turn on you to shoot you, it makes it harder for him. Some people get pissed off at you for standing way back like that, but so what?"

Radio: "14, 415 South Park. Suspicious persons."

Maillett picked up the mike and said simply: "Ten-4."

Radio: "14. We've been advised its an SLA house. 12, Code 9 unit 14 at 415 South Park."

Booker smiled.

"She's not kidding," Maillett said seriously.

Booker stepped harder on the gas.

"You've got to turn right here, go past the island and hang a U-turn," Maillett calmly explained to the inexperienced cop.

At the location, Booker stopped the unit in the middle of the street, two houses down from the address. Curtains were drawn on all the windows of the stucco house. No one was visible anywhere on the premises. Booker and Maillett were the first police officers on the scene. If indeed this was a hideout for the infamous Symbionese Liberation Army, then they would undoubtedly have their hands full.

They both approached the house carefully, keeping a good distance between each other, so that it would take more than one shotgun blast to get them both. They checked the sides of the house, then Maillett rapped on the front door while Booker stood off to one side. Both officers had their hands on their gun stocks, and Maillett stood away from the door so that if a bullet was fired through the door it would not hit him. The door opened slightly, and a tall, slender black peered out suspiciously at the officers. As the door opened wider, a young black boy was visible behind the taller youth.

"Do you gentlemen live here?" Maillett asked.

They nodded their heads in unison. "What do you want?" the older one asked with an edge in his voice.

"We received a call that there were suspicious persons here. May we come in and have a look?"

"Yes," the younger boy said.

"No," the older one quickly and somewhat belligerently countered.

Maillett walked in the house, followed closely by Booker. Maillett went through the living room, into the kitchen, and directed Booker to check the bedrooms. The rookie cop hesitated for a moment, then proceeded to the bedrooms in a careful, controlled walk. By this time the older youth was screaming that the cops had no right being in his house; finally, disgusted, he fled out the front door. The two officers met in the family room at the back of the house. Maillett pulled back the curtains. Two men dressed in black stood in the backyard with pistols in their hands. It took everyone in the house a split second to realize that the two men wore badges. They were Unit 12, the backup unit.

Back in the living room, Maillett explained to the older youth, who had returned by then, why they entered his house. "Your brother, who lives here, too, gave us permission. If he had said no, then we wouldn't have come in."

While Maillett talked, the television—with the volume turned down—was broadcasting the news story of the year. But none of the officers in the room were aware of it.

Once in the car, Booker explained to Maillett why he hesitated in the house. "I've been told in the academy not to separate from my partner."

"Sometimes it's necessary," Maillett answered.

"Something I always do with the person I ride with is to tell them that if we separate in a house and someone pulls a gun or knife on him, and tells him to call his partner, that he should call me by his first name. And if the same thing happened to me, I would call him by my first name. That way we'll know what to expect."

• • •

Back at the station to pick up their jackets for what was rapidly becoming a chilly summer evening, Maillett and Booker first learned of the fiery SLA-police shoot out going on in Los Angeles a few miles to the north.

"L.A.P.D. has put out a call for fragmentation grenades," one officer regaled. "They're gonna blow the whole fucking block up!"

"Cinque tried to run from the burning house, but the bullets on his shoulder caught fire and blew him all to hell," another officer claimed.

"That really breaks my heart," offered patrolman Robert Oroscoe in mock sadness.

"Isn't that something," someone else said. "The SLA is in San Francisco for months and the police can't find them at all. They come down here and in a few days L.A.P.D. blows them up. S.F.P.D. is really going to be pissed."

That night, the Compton P.D. received a bomb threat. Also, the dire warning that five police officers would be killed for every dead SLA member was made public by a radical group. Three police sharpshooters spent the night on the roof of the Compton headquarters. Just in case.

• • •

Meanwhile, Maillett and Booker must complete their watch. Back on patrol, they immediately receive a suspicious person call. Radio: "One male white, with long blond hair. Standing at the corner of. . . ."

"I guess a lone white male in this area would be suspicious," agrees Maillett.

After a quiet hour during which the two hungry officers gratefully eat a large spaghetti dinner while flirting with the restaurant owner's cute waitress-daughter, Maillett begins another story, for the benefit of both the rookie cop and the writer.

"I'll tell you a weird one. This couple had been married for 15 years. One night in bed the husband made the wife suck his dick. . . . She'd never done that before. Then he says it's his turn, he's going to eat her. He does. Afterwards, he's stretched out on the bed, you know, feeling pretty good. She gets up out of bed and goes to the closet and takes out their .22 pistol. She loads it, right there in front of him, and says she is going to shoot him. He says, 'Go ahead, bitch.' Then she blows a hole in the back of his head. He was dead by the time we got over there."

While cruising in the industrial part of town, the squad car approaches an intersection and slows as the officers spot a car parked against a curb at an unusual angle. Somebody is behind the wheel, apparently trying to start the car. Booker pulls up behind the vehicle, and

Maillett flashes the unit's spotlight on the occupant. He turns around, and his large, dopey, almost-unseeing eyes tell the story.

"A duce," Maillett says disgustedly. "A damn duce."

"A what?" I ask.

"A duce means a drunk driver," Maillett explains. "It also means we're going to be tied up for quite awhile."

When the officers get out, the man has his car engine going, but he isn't aware of it. He keeps grinding the starter.

"Turn the engine off and get out," Maillett orders the man, who has blood running down his face. The driver's only response is a feeble attempt to get the car in gear. Maillett goes immediately to the driver's door and opens it. "Get out!" he yells. "Don't you understand English?!"

The man struggles out from behind the wheel and as he stands up next to the car, Maillett backs away. "Walk over to me," the officer says.

The drunk manages to take a few comical, struggling steps before falling flat on his face in the road.

As Booker turns off the man's car ignition and looks the vehicle over, Maillett goes to the squad car and takes out a small Instamatic camera. He takes several flashcube pictures as the confused man half-sits on the asphalt. "These are for me to take to court when he tries to say that he wasn't drunk."

Booker and Maillett check the skid marks on the pavement and figure out that the man has simply steered into the curb, knocked into a utility pole, and spun around in the intersection to end up where he did—apparently with no help from any other traffic. In short, it's a nice piece of drunken driving.

"It . . . weren't my fault," the white man protests.

"Yeah, those telephone poles are really hard to avoid," Maillett agrees.

While Booker calls for a tow truck, Maillett handcuffs the man's hands behind his back and helps him into the backseat of the patrol car. He reaches into the man's trouser pocket to find identification, then quickly pulls his hand out when he realizes the pants are urine-soaked.

"Jesus, you pissed your pants!" The officer puts on his gloves before reaching back into the man's pocket to take out a wallet.

"What's your name?" Maillett asks.

"Jasmeahhschoondoll."

"What?"

"Jasmondschoooondell."

Reading the identification in the wallet, Maillett asks: "Is your name James Scondle?"

The man nods his head.

"We'll have to take him to the hospital to have that cut sewed up," Maillett informs Booker.

"Yeah, he must have hit his head on the steering wheel."

Just then a call comes over the radio for units to respond to an in-progress 459. "Jesus, that's right down the block," Booker exclaims. "We could be down there catching some burglars if it wasn't for this duce!"

"Haveto . . . goto . . . baffroom," the man said from the backseat.

"Look, James, you'll have to hold it," said Maillett. "I'm not going to take those handcuffs off. And there's no way I'm going to hold your dick for you to take a leak."

"Our car is going to smell nice for the rest of the

night," Booker observed wryly.

At the hospital, the man's forehead was sewn up with several stitches. While the doctor was doing his work, Maillett nodded at me standing nearby and said: "Watch it, doctor. This guy is writing a book about us. He's checking out your work."

The young doctor with modishly long hair looked curiously at me for a moment, then said, "My name is John Smith. Be sure you spell it right."

After the stitches were in, the doctor checked the man over for any other injuries. "He's just intoxicated," the doctor finally pronounced.

The man refused to take any of the three drunk tests that Maillett offered. The officer wrote "refused" on the proper sheet and said: "That's your decision. I told you, your license will be automatically suspended for refusing. And those judges! Boy, they just love getting a hold of somebody who has refused."

The man was then taken to the X-ray room, and while the officers waited outside the open door, a small, wiry X-ray technician struggled with the drunk, trying to get him into the proper positions for head and back X rays. Every once in a while she turned her head away, unable to stomach the smell of the urine-soaked clothes. Maillett went into the room a couple of times and harshly ordered the man into the proper position.

Some 30 minutes later the technician delivered the X rays to the doctor's desk in the emergency ward. The doctor was busy with another patient, and Maillett, who was sitting nearby, walked over to the desk and picked up the X rays. He studied the skull shot for several seconds, then moaned.

"You have a calcium deposit on your brain," Maillett said to the drunk. "But don't worry about it, Mr. Scondle."

"Oh, sure," the drunk said, cracking up at the cop.

Later, after the doctor had released the man, Booker and Maillett booked him into the Compton jail and wrote their lengthy reports. When they got back on the street, it was two hours after they had first spotted the drunk. One duce had tied up their two-man unit for that long. And on this particular night, the Maillett-Booker team represented about 20% of the law enforcement protection in the City of Compton.

●　●　●

The next afternoon Patrolman Raymond Maillett started his 10-hour shift as a one-man unit. Usually the units don't become two-man until nightfall. But sometimes—when there is a shortage of regular and reserve officers—there are some one-man units out all night. The policemen don't like that at all. They note statistics that show most cop fatalities occur in single-man units. But this Saturday afternoon, Maillett, who is normally a mellow guy anyway, wasn't complaining much. The weather was clear and warm and he was looking forward to having the next three days off. Like most of the other Compton patrolmen, however, Maillett was wearing an extra gun this day.

"Because of the SLA thing yesterday," he explained. "We were advised in briefing it would be a good idea to have a backup gun on us. Just in case we stop someone who gets the drop on us, and we have to throw down our service revolver."

Maillett was carrying a small 9-mm automatic pistol under his belt. It was slightly smaller than a .38; with good penetrating power but not-so-good stopping power. "It's good for shooting through cars when someone is trying to get away," he said.

Also in briefing, the officers were drilled on what they should do if their partner has a gun pointed to his head and they are ordered to drop their gun on the ground. "Do not do so," the sergeant said. "The threat of your gun is what is keeping your partner alive—to be used as a shield. If you drop your gun, you'll both be killed."

It was left to the individual officers to work out with their partners whether or not they wanted their partners to try to shoot the gunman in such an incident. "I always tell my partner to shoot," said one officer. "I'll drop down and get out of the way as best as I can. But shoot the fucker so he doesn't kill anyone else."

On the way to the back lot to get into a patrol car, Maillett and I stopped and talked to Patrolman Robert Quintana. I asked him about his bulletproof vest, and he unbuttoned the top two buttons of his uniform and proudly displayed the thick, white nylon-encased vest.

"The only thing it won't stop is a .41 magnum," Quintana said in his heavily accented, machine-gun style delivery. "But a .22 and .38, it will stop like that! I can hardly wait to get up off the ground and kill the mother-fucker who tries to shoot me! You know, like Supercop."

His black eyes suddenly became intense. "Some people call me chicken because I wear it! But I'm no chicken! If I was I wouldn't be a cop! You know what I mean? This vest. It just gives me a little bit better odds."

On our first cruise around town, Maillett pointed out the intersection of School Street and Wilmington. "That's where I got shot," he explained. "I was standing there by that pole. The bullet came from that green house across the street."

We passed another patrol unit that was parked on a side street. Patrolman Robert Oroscoe was checking himself out in the rear-view mirror, combing his hair.

"You look all right," Maillett said into the radio mike.

"Roger," Oroscoe replied over the radio in a businesslike voice.

Seconds later, while we were waiting at a red light, Oroscoe quickly came up behind us and stepped on it as the light turned green. Oroscoe, talking on his outside speaker, said as he passed us: "Give me some."

Maillett busted up. "That's an inside joke in the police department. It means give me some ass."

Within minutes the radio cracked in serious business. A 245 (assault with a deadly weapon) had come down several blocks away, and the suspects were fleeing the scene in a purple car. Before we had gone two blocks another unit reported it had pulled over the suspected car. We provided backup.

When Maillett pulled up, two officers had two blacks spread-eagled on their purple Ford Mustang. A block away, across some railroad tracks, we saw a crowd gathering around two police cars. The victim, an old lady who lived in a nearby mental institution, was down on the ground. The officers decided to transport the suspects across the railroad tracks, and see if the lady could identify them.

The two young suspects, both husky blacks, were

taking the incident in a surprisingly light-hearted way; smiling and laughing to themselves. By the time they were taken over to the other side of the railroad tracks and escorted out of a police car, the old lady was sitting in the ambulance with a medic attending to her wound.

"You better quit smiling, fucker," one officer said softly to one of the suspects. "This isn't funny."

Patrolman Quintana moved his face within an inch of one of the suspects, and looking menacingly into his eyes, said: "What have you been arrested for?" The suspect told him of several prior arrests.

Not moving his face away, Quintana said simply: "You should be executed for that."

A middle-aged white man dressed in a suit came over to the police and said he was the manager of the home the lady stayed at. He said he had heard that the lady had attempted to assist the female in a boyfriend-girl friend fight, and was rewarded for her efforts by having a bottle smashed against her head. The ambulance attendant signaled the police, and each suspect was brought over individually. The tired, disturbed, bloody old lady was unable or unwilling to identify either of them. The men were cut loose. And the ambulance took the elderly victim to the hospital.

Not long after we cleared on the assault call, we got a residential burglary in-progress call. Things were really picking up now. This obviously wasn't going to be a quiet Saturday afternoon for Ray Maillett.

With gun in hand, Maillett walked in the open side door to the neat, well-cared-for house. Another officer, also with gun in hand, was in front of him. The first officer peeled off to the left, to go through the kitchen. Maillett headed for the living room. The house was deadly quiet. Every time he turned a blind corner, Maillett thrust the gun ahead, ready to blast a potential assailant.

The house was empty. The entry point was obviously a smashed bedroom window, which had spots of blood mixed in with the broken glass. When Maillett finally opened the front door, it looked as if the neighborhood had been taken over by the Compton Police. There were six patrol units parked outside. "This is Code 4," Maillett said to some officers. (Code 4: No help needed; everything is okay.)

Maillett was left on the scene to fill out a burglary report. The teen-age daughter, who was a student at Compton Junior College, said she came home first. She always comes in the side door, she explained. Only this time it was ajar. She pushed it open and took a step into the house, then she saw the young stranger in the living room. They must have scared each other equally. She ran out the side door to a neighbor's, where she called the police. He obviously hurriedly exited out the bedroom window, ripping some flesh en route.

"If I didn't stop at the hamburger stand I probably would have been here when he came in," the still-shaking girl remarked.

The mother and father had arrived home during the apparent police siege. "Man, when I saw all those cop cars I thought maybe it was SLA here," the man said. "They on the run, you know. Could be looking for someplace to stay."

"All I know is that I'm going to get me a big dog," said the mother.

"Too bad I wasn't here with my Big 16," the father

said, then immediately jumped up to make sure his loaded shotgun was still in the bedroom closet. It was. In fact, nothing seemed to be missing from the well-furnished home. Apparently the burglar was interrupted during the early stages of his crime.

"Some night I going to sit here with all the lights off and wait for him to come back," the father said. "Then I'm going to get him with my shotgun."

The mother grimaced slightly, while Maillett was unresponsive, finishing the report. He said later: "When people talk like that, I don't even answer them. It's just too stupid to respond to."

Midway through the watch, Maillett stopped at a favorite dairy drive-in. "I love chocolate milk," he said, as he brought two quarts and handed me one. We both promptly spilled some of the milk from the full bottles down the front of us. We cleaned ourselves off with a large handkerchief, then drank the cool, sweet liquid.

"Good," I said. "Thanks a lot."

"Yeah, sure," Maillett said. "Hey, I know what we can do tonight. I'll see if I can't find a peter party for you."

"A what?"

"Peter party. You know, people screwing. It's really funny. Sometimes, you put a light on them and they don't stop. One night I caught this couple screwing in a park, and chased them out. Later, I drove through another park and there they were, getting it on. I chased them away again. That poor guy. He must have been in pain."

7

STAKEOUT

"A black and white unit is a deterrent at that particular moment. But as soon as you clear the area, a crime will happen. In an unmarked car, you hope to catch them in the act."

—Officer Tommy Johnson, Robbery, Compton P.D.

"The spiraling intensity of the crime problem has proven particularly acute in cities experiencing rapid urbanization and accelerating population growth. The City of Compton is no exception to this national trend. In fact, few cities in the United States, if any, have a worse crime problem as that which the City of Compton now faces. The crime problems of most cities, by comparison, might seem to be relative Utopias.

"Compton has the highest incidence of major crimes per 100,000 population in the state, when measured by the FBI (Part 1) Crime Index. The incident of robbery has been one of the major crime problems in Compton. . . . There has been a 71% increase in robberies from January, 1969, to January, 1973."

So reads the introduction to the grant proposal submitted by the Compton Police Department in order to receive $100,000 of state money for a crime specific (robbery) unit. The thinking behind such a program is that the grant will pay the salaries of the officers involved in the unit, as well as the specialized equipment that is needed. The unit will then spend full time trying to reduce and prevent their specific crime—in this case, robbery. (Compton also has a similar grant for burglary, which it received nearly three years ago.)

Sergeant Jim Fette, a 15-year veteran of the Compton P.D., is in charge of the four-man robbery unit. The others are Tommy Johnson and AI Preston, both of whom are special investigators (trained in evidence gathering, such as fingerprints, etc.), and arms expert Dennis Ford, who doubles as the "reappropriation" expert. (Translation: he begs, borrows or steals from other parts of the police station anything the robbery unit needs. Remember Ford? He's the officer who got pissed on by the drunk while on a narcotics stakeout.)

The robbery unit was only a month or so old when I visited it, and Fette and his men hadn't yet received their equipment. Eventually, they will be able to wire up 10 or 12 businesses (that they have projected may be robbed) with special electronic alarms that go directly to the team's mobile units parked a few blocks away. That way, hopefully, they will crash in on in-progress robberies. Ideally, their response time will be considerably less that

60 seconds—and some three to five times faster than a patrol car cruising in another area could make it. Other cities that have similar programs (Oakland, San Diego, and Ingle wood) have discovered that their specific robbery units tend to get into a lot of gunfights.

"They must think we'll get into something," explained Fette. "We have bulletproof vests on order. I've got three good men [30 patrolmen applied for the program], and as soon as we get our equipment, we'll catch some robbers and deter some others."

Unlike the overworked specific burglary unit, the robbery boys will have no normal case load responsibilities. That means that their days won't be taken up in routine investigations and report-writing, but they will be free for stakeouts and other field work.

The "in" places to rob in Compton now are drive-in food stands and drive-in cleaners. Liquor stores are out. "We haven't had a liquor store robbed in years," said Fette. "What happened was that all the owners got guns and started shooting robbers. The word is out now that liquor stores aren't worth it because you might get shot."

On a recent Friday night, the robbery unit beefed its numbers up with reserves and put 10 men on four stakeouts: two Jack-in-the-Boxes and two fried chicken places. Nothing came down.

Then, the next night, one of the chicken stands was robbed. "Damn, if we had our equipment, that place would have been wired up," Fette asserted.

There is one robber the cops want really bad. He is believed responsible for five robberies in the month of April alone, and he always uses a silver .32 caliber revolver. His M.O. is donut shop robberies. Surprisingly, he has robbed the same place twice. Then, unbelievably, the next week he came by to see the manager about a job. The manager thought he recognized him when they were talking, and as soon as the man left, the manager called the police. The manager also had the guy fill out a job application. He left his real name and real address. Unbelievable.

"We're going to try to bring him in today," Fette said. "Johnson and Preston are going out to see if he's home."

AI Preston has been on the police force for three years. He didn't enter police work until the relatively late age of 29. He is a tall, black man with closely cropped hair. He hails from "the great state of Louisiana" and spent two years in the airborne Army—six months of it in combat in Vietnam. "Police work is something I've always wanted to do," explained Preston. "So I took the exam and went through with it. I'm quite pleased with police work, although it can be frustrating at times."

Tommy Johnson, a young black man, has been on the Compton force almost five years, spending two years in the narcotics unit. He's one of the few Compton officers who actually lives in Compton. "I volunteered for this [robbery] duty because I'd like to catch some of these guys in the act and be able to personally testify against them in court," Johnson said. "That will be a real change instead of the normal way of doing things, where you have to find witnesses, hold an investigation and try to convict them on hearsay evidence."

Johnson said he believes once the robbery unit gets its mobile units and electronic alarms they will be able to stop most of the commercial robberies in town. "The San Diego specific robbery [unit] statistics show that the average armed robber needs only 30 seconds to get the money and leave the place of business. The way our alarm-stakeout system will be set up, we'll be on the scene 10 to 15 seconds after the alarm is in."

Preston pointed out that the robbery suspect's house was in the next block. "He's a big dude, 190 lbs., short and stocky. He'll go 148 [resisting arrest]. We'll probably have to kill his ass. He's been arrested before, for grand theft auto and assaulting an officer."

At the house, Johnson knocked on the front door while Preston covered the house. No one answered, but soon an older lady came in sight walking down the sidewalk with a broom in her hand. She was the suspect's mother. No, she said, her son was not home.

"This is in reference to a stolen auto report," Johnson lied.

"Oh, yes, my son's car was stolen," the lady said.

"Well, we'll check back with you later."

"He hasn't been home for three or four days," she explained. "But he called his father and told him to report that his car had been stolen. That's why we called you."

"Yes, well, we'll check back later."

"Thank you, officers."

Back in the car, Johnson explained: "The guy knew his car was made on the robbery, so he left town and called home to have his old man report to us that his car had been stolen earlier that day. So we're pretending to investigate the stolen car report."

Johnson and Preston made a sweep around the town's commercial areas, pointing out the hot spots for recent robberies.

"So many people are burglarized and robbed in

this city, it's really frustrating," Johnson admitted. "Of all the latent fingerprints I've taken and of all the stacks of paper work in the last five years, I've only been in court two times to testify against someone. After a while, you just don't think what you are doing is doing much good. That's why I'm really excited about this program. It will be such a thrill to catch someone in the act. I mean, what a thrill to roll up on a guy when he's leaving the scene of an armed robbery. We'll get into a lot of shoot-outs. Eventually, we'll have disguises and work in some of the businesses as employees. We'll have meetings with businessmen to explain the program. We won't have any problem finding volunteers for our alarms. There'll probably be a long waiting list."

Cruising through the parking lot of a large shopping center, Johnson observed wryly: "A single lady in this parking lot stands a 75% chance of getting her purse snatched. A security guard was killed here a couple months ago by a purse snatcher, but not before he shot and killed the other guy."

The call is armed robbery at a liquor store. The first cops on the scene, not taking any chances, order everyone outside the store to get down on the pavement.

An arrest following a street knifing.

• • •

Burglary is the most common crime in Compton. There are 350 burglaries a month in Compton; an average of more than ten each day. The crime specific unit has been in operation almost three years. Unlike the new robbery unit, the burg detail is not free of routine paper work and investigation. Although an original grant proposal called for such a situation, once the department received the federal funds for the program it couldn't resist the temptation of handing the unit all the burglary responsibility, thereby freeing other detectives from such work.

Chief Cochée and Lt. Art Taylor study a map pinpointing burglary-robbery incidents in Compton.

Sgt. A. Camarillo, head of the burglary unit, estimated that 65% of the five-man team's time is taken up with investigations and follow-up, 20% community awareness (stressing to residents the importance of lock bolts, etc.), and about 10% surveillance.

Camarillo and some of his burg unit headed for the

local topless joint, the Red Garter, one day after work. Surprisingly, the place has a good reputation, and many cops frequent the beer bar and watch the young girls—all of them white—undulate to the jukebox music. There are usually three to four girls on duty, and they take turns dancing to two or three numbers. The first song they dance to with their bikini outfit on, they take off their tops for the second one, and on the third one—no, they don't take off the bottom anymore because it's recently been made illegal, but the third routine is quite nice.

"Hey, Anna, do a good dance for our friend here," Camarillo yelled to the brunette on the stage who had just taken her top off. "He'll write a book about you."

Anna smiled and began undulating all over the "stage."

"We call her Anna Banana," Camarillo said, as he forked over money for a second pitcher of beer. "Look at her nose and you'll see why. God, she is so dumb! She can't even hold a normal conversation."

Camarillo, a tall, barrel-chested white officer with long hair modishly styled over his ears, turned his attention back to the stage. "Oh, Anna Banana. You're lookin' good. You lost some weight, uh? Look nice, Anna. . . ."

When Anna was through with the dance and had her top back on, she walked by our table on the way to her bar duties.

"Hey, Anna, my friend here needs a little action," Camarillo joked.

Anna Banana's lips spread into a wide smile under her long nose.

"Where's Bobby?" Camarillo asked.

"Who?" she said.

"Oh, come on, Anna. What time is Bobby picking you up?"

She shrugged her shoulders as if totally confused, and walked away to hustle beer.

"Bobby is her black pimp," Camarillo explained. "He takes her to work and picks her up at night. She doesn't even own a car. We're always giving her a bad time about staying here until he comes to pick her up, then busting him. I understand she goes for $10."

• • •

Detectives Brent Nielsen and Jim Pearson of the burg unit are sitting in the unit's new green van, parked in front of a Compton furniture store. The officers, both white, are waiting for a store employee to get off work. They suspect he is responsible for the theft of some $10,000 worth of color TV sets at the store. They have alerted the manager to the possibility of an inside job, but have asked that the employee be allowed to keep his job and his suspicions not be aroused so the cops can tail him and try to find the merchandise, or catch him in the act of another burglary.

Sitting on surveillance is one of the more boring aspects of the job. Shooting the bull is a must in order to kill time.

"We've had some real winners who were patrolmen on this department," said Pearson, an accomplished storyteller. "This one guy really took the cake. He was a bachelor, and he used to practically live out of his station locker. Before he got dressed he'd smell all the dirty socks he kept in a pile at the bottom of the locker, to see which ones were the least dirty. Then he'd rinse out his mouth with mouthwash, and spit it back into the bottle. He got jacked up by L.A.P.D. for carrying a gun in his swim trunks. He didn't have any I.D. on him, and they just couldn't believe he was a police officer. Can you imagine having a gun sticking out of your swim trunks on a public beach? We had another guy who was a chronic sleeper. He would fall asleep in the middle of writing a report. One morning at eight o'clock another patrol car passed through an intersection and right in the middle of the left lane, blocking traffic, this guy had his unit stopped. He was sound asleep. Apparently he had stopped for a red light and dropped off."

When the radio broadcasts a 211 in-progress at a Jack-in-the-Box only two minutes away, Pearson suddenly comes to attention.

"What do you think, Brent?' he asks. "Want to respond ?"

"If we do, we might lose this guy," says Nielsen.

"Guess I'm a patrolman at heart," Pearson says, settling back for more stories. "We have this sergeant on the department," he continues, "who did a bunch of research and planning on how safe the .45 automatic is. Of course, everyone knows the kind of stopping power it has, but a lot of cops don't trust a .45 because they fire when they're not suppose to. Anyway, the sergeant did a good job on his report, and he ended up convincing the chief that we should switch over to .45s (from .357s) for our standard-issue weapon. The day the .45s arrived, the sergeant had a box of them in an upstairs interrogation room, and he was trying to fit one in its holster, and it went off by mistake. The bullet went through the wall and into the dick [detectives] room. Captain Correa almost had a heart attack, he yelled for everyone to hit the deck. Everyone in the room thought they were under siege. When the sergeant came in to see if anyone was hit, he looked slightly ill."

"Jimmy, here comes two guys out the front," says Nielsen from the front passenger's seat where he is slumped down.

Pearson, who is in the back of the van, lying on the carpeted floor, gets up and looks cautiously out the side window. "I think that fat guy is our man. The manager is supposed to come out and wipe his face with a handkerchief right after the guy comes out."

"Yeah, okay, here's the manager now," says Nielsen. The signal is given, although the manager, who doesn't know the van is parked across the street in a busy shopping center parking lot, doesn't seem quite sure that anyone is receiving his signal. He stands around outside longer than he should, and keeps wiping his face. "Jesus, he's trying to find us. Go back inside, man."

"There in that small parking lot," Pearson says. "I can't see what they're getting into. Let's move."

Nielsen, driving, pulls the van across the street. Pearson stays down out of sight. (One man alone looks less suspicious than two.) "They're pulling out in a red pickup," Nielsen reports. "Our guy is in the passenger's seat. Okay, you can come up, Jimmy. We've got a few cars between us."

"Our guy's house is only a few blocks away," says Pearson. "The manager said the guy in the pickup usually takes him home. That's probably where they're going now."

The man gets out in front of his house, and the pickup takes off. Our van pulls over to the curb several houses away. The man jumps into an old white car sitting in his driveway, and takes off, with the van following not far behind.

"This is our plan," Pearson explains. "When we talked to the guy at work today, we told him we suspected it was an inside job. We didn't finger him, but we made it clear we were closing in. We hope that we rattled him enough so that he'll try to move the stuff, maybe to get rid of it."

The van follows the truck across Compton, running two or three red lights in order to stay up with him. Inevitably, the suspect's car hits the tail end of a green light, and the time we get to the intersection, it's run. Pearson looks to the right and says "go" when it's clear, and Nielsen checks the left, then blows the light. (Unlike on TV, people who are tailing someone don't stay glued to the guy's bumper.)

The car pulls into a mammoth new housing project that looks like an expensive apartment complex. "You ought to see the way these new places are getting torn up already," Pearson comments. "It's our ghetto of the future."

Nielsen parks the van at the curb, covering the only exit to the parking area the suspect drove into. More waiting. And waiting.

"We must look pretty suspicious," says Nielsen. "Three white dudes in a van. I expect the residents to call the sheriff because the SLA is parked in front of their apartments. The sheriff will probably come out and jack us up."

Several cars come out of the parking area, but none of them are the suspect's car. Finally, Nielsen says, "If he doesn't move in a few minutes, let's pick any car to follow. I figure one out of three of these people are crooks."

"Yeah," says Pearson, "the odds are with you."

More stories. "Some officers shot a lieutenant's cat out in the parking lot," Pearson relates, "and they put it under the wheel of our van to make it look like we ran over it. The lieutenant was smarter than that, though. . . .

"Not long ago one of our patrolmen responded to a 459 at a liquor store that had been getting knocked off quite a bit. What happened was that the owner's grandson was closing the store up, and he accidentally tripped the alarm. He had a bag of money and a gun in his hand when the cop said, 'Hold it!' The kid, thinking it was a robbery, fired the gun over his shoulder. The cop shot him in the head with his .357 magnum, and killed him on the spot.

"We have a Latin patrolman on the force who really scares me," Pearson continues. "He got this call that an old man had been knocked over in front of a store. The old man told him that a Black Muslim who had been selling pies in front of the store knocked him down when he wouldn't buy one. The Muslims had gone back to their headquarters, so this cop gets the old man in his car and drives him to the storefront. I was on patrol then, and I got a Code 9 call at the Muslim storefront. About the time I get there this officer is standing in front of the storefront's plate glass window with his shotgun. He jacks a round in the chamber and orders everybody out of the storefront.

I'm thinking, Ok, fuck, this is it! Twenty Muslims come out, and the last guy out looks over the scene. By now there were three or four cops out front. This leader yells, 'Front,' and each cop suddenly has three Muslims standing right over him. If they had decided to take us, we would have been wiped out. The old man points out the two guys who knocked him down and, luckily, the leader tells them to go with the police. It was really a hairy scene for a while. I believe the patrolman who arranged the confrontation could single-handedly start another Watts Riot." (Author's note: The patrolman mentioned in this sequence is no longer with the department.)

Finally, near midnight, Pearson and Nielsen get bored and decide to find some other action.

"It's way past curfew," Nielsen says. "Let's go jack up some juveniles."

• • •

Cruising slowly through a residential neighborhood that is nearly pitch-black on this moonlit night, Pearson eyes a youth walking alone down the sidewalk. We pass him, and then see two more juveniles following, about a block behind. Nielsen whips the van around, and Pearson jumps out the side.

"Okay," Pearson orders, "hands on the truck. Come on." To the kid a block away, who has started to walk back in our direction, he yells: "You too." When the three boys, ages 12, 15 and 17 have their hands on the van, Nielsen checks them for weapons.

"I've seen all you boys before," says Nielsen. "What have I arrested you for?" he asks the 17-year-old.

"Robbery," the youth answers.

"And you?" to the 15-year-old.

"Burglary."

"And you?" to the 12-year-old.

"You didn't arrest me."

"Somebody did. What for?"

"Shooting into a house."

"What are you boys doing out on the street two hours after curfew?" asks Nielsen.

"Goin' to the store."

"Yeah, right. You are looking for a house to rob."

"No, man, we were going to the store."

"What store?"

"Any store."

"The nearest store open this time at night is miles away," Nielsen says, keeping one up on the kids. "You know what I think we should do with them?" he says to Pearson. "Let's take them into the hills and call Firestone."

All three kids show righteous fear in their eyes. They know full well that if the L.A. sheriff deputies from the nearby Firestone precinct catch up with them at this time of night, they'll get the shit beat out of them.

"No, please, sir!"

"Ahh, don't do that. We'll go home!"

"Pleeasse don't!"

Nielsen keeps a serious look, but he is obviously having fun. "All right, everyone head in a different direction, and get home," he orders. "We're going to be riding around here all night, and if we see you again, we're going to throw you in the van and call Firestone. And you know what they'll do to you. All right, take off! You've got 30 seconds to get out of my sight."

The kids scramble in three different directions, obviously intent upon seeking the protection of their homes—at least for this night.

Back in the van, Nielsen is happy with the confrontation. "You know what, Jimmy? We just prevented a robbery."

The burglary van takes off into the black night, looking for more action.

BRUCE HENDERSON

8

SUPERCOP

"The street people think there's a bunch of pussies in this department."

—Patrolman Victor Guerrero, Compton P.D.

Patrolman Vic Guerrero, a handsome, muscular Puerto Rican, is the Super Macho Fantasy come true. He races motorcycles, drives a hopped-up Corvette, scuba dives, plans to take up skydiving and has a black belt in karate.

He is not at all happy about what he thinks is the soft reputation of the Compton police force, and whenever possible he tries to change that image by kicking some ass.

"I'll tell you what I consider my greatest compliment," he said. "I got called to this gang-fight incident. When they saw the cops, the guys scattered in different directions. Me and my partner went after them, one by one. When I caught up with one, I asked him how old he was. If they were over 16, I told them that's old enough to get their ass kicked. I'd hit them once in the stomach, and they'd double over. Then I went and found another one. Well, a few weeks later, I went to a 'shots fired' call. The reserve I was riding with was a real dumb shit. I told him not to talk to me and not to touch the radio, even if I got shot. I just wanted the guy to leave me alone to do my thing. I tell the reserve to stay in the car and I get out and knock on the door of the house where the shots were supposed to be coming from. A guy answers the door and I tell him why I'm there, and he tells me nothing happened here. I say, 'Okay, can I use your phone to call my station ?' I walk in the house and there are about 10 to 15 guys there; all of them in the early twenties or so. Some are a lot bigger than me. While I'm dialing the phone, a couple guys start making a move on me, saying, 'What the fuck is this pig doing here?' One of the guys suddenly says, 'Hey, wait! This cop's crazy! He's the one who knocked me out with one punch. Don't go near him.' They all backed off."

There are similar incidents Guerrero is proud to relate. There's this Mexican bar in town that used to have fights, knifings, and shootings all the time. None of the cops wanted to go near the place unless they had to, and then only if they had a partner along. Guerrero started walking through it alone, picking fights whenever possible. It took him about six fights, and that was it. No more trouble. Now, when he goes into the bar, everyone in the kitchen, the bartender, and owner are happy to see him. Guerrero's last incident at the bar involved a big guy who wanted to fight him. The guy told Vic he wouldn't be such a big shit with his gun off. Guerrero handed his gun to a bar employee and went outside with the big troublemaker. The bar emptied as everyone went outside to watch. As they were squaring off, Guerrero karate-kicked the guy's hat right off his head. He did it so fast the big guy turned around, thinking that someone from behind had knocked his hat off. He couldn't believe it when no one was behind him. The spectators laughed, and the big guy lost his stomach for fighting.

Although Guerrero's tactics make him somewhat controversial within the department (and indeed within the community)., even the officers who are critical of his style name Guerrero as the guy they would want backing them up in a tough situation. In one backup situation, a punk let loose with a mean swing aimed at an officer's head, and Guerrero stopped his hand in mid-air, and chopped him down with one mighty karate thrust.

A patrol sergeant recently broke up the team of Guerrero and Patrolman Ron Dillworth, a muscular black officer who was recently selected by his fellow officers as the best patrolman of the year. "The sergeant thought we were too rough. He called me 'Sudden Death' and Dillworth '60 Days in the Hospital.' I guess it was just as well anyway, because Dillworth's heart couldn't take riding with me two nights in a row. He'd get mad at me for driving so fast, and would go all night without talking to me."

Guerrero's fellow cops rate him as the fastest driver on the force. Not the safest fast driver; there's a significant difference. Although he can handle a car very well, his driving does tend to support the contention of some that Vic Guerrero has a death wish. Even on nonemergency calls, he takes turns as if they were the final lap of a championship Grand Prix race. One night, when Patrolman Jack McConnell was Guerrero's partner, Vic was speeding suicidally to a call when McConnell reached over and turned off the ignition key. He then quickly threw the key out the window. "I couldn't take any more of that shit," explained McConnell.

Guerrero talks in glowing terms about the reputation of the county sheriff's department. "They kick ass," he says admiringly. "The saying on the street is: '77th (precinct, L.A.P.D.) will blow you up, Firestone will kick your ass, Compton is all right.'"

Firestone is the local station for the county sheriff's department. Their patrols crisscross the heavily black neighborhoods of unincorporated Watts and Compton, which has many intersections and streets that come under county jurisdiction. The sheriff has an elite corps, called S.E.B.—Special Enforcement Bureau. They wear riot helmets all the time, and reportedly the way deputies are chosen for S.E.B. is by their being good ass-kickers. (All the S.E.B. units I saw were lily white.) Guerrero said he's seen gang members giving Compton cops a bad time in a touchy street scene, but when a Firestone patrol car cruises into the situation, the word goes out quickly: "Firestone! Take off! Cool it! Firestone!" Guerrero said Firestone has the gang punks trained so well that when one of their cars cruises slowly down a neighborhood street, the gang guys come up and put their hands on the hood of the police car in the traditional frisk position. The gang members also know that if they run from Firestone they will probably not get arrested, but they will definitely get the shit kicked out of them. "The Firestone guys figure that anyone who is running is guilty of something, so they kick his ass and leave him where he falls," Guerrero explained. "That way they don't have to fill out any paper work." In particularly tough situations, the Compton cops even use the threat of Firestone. "If you don't cool it, we'll call Firestone," they are known to warn.

"There's this one Firestone deputy who has a portable tape recorder in his car, and when he gets a Code 3 call he turns on the William Tell Overture and plays it over his loudspeaker," Guerrero said laughingly. "That's his siren. I've seen him pull up to a gang fight and have everyone on both sides start cracking up. Wouldn't that make a great scene in a police film?"

(Chief Cochée is very aware of the reputation of Firestone. When he heard recently that Firestone units were randomly stopping and harassing people within Compton city limits, he ordered that the county sheriff turn over a written report every time they make a stop in Compton city limits. For the time being, the most blatant harassment incidents stopped.)

When asked who he thinks is the best patrolman in the department, Guerrero names Ron Malachi,, a big, soft-spoken black man who is a decorated Vietnam combat veteran. Malachi was nominated for the Congressional Medal of Honor but received the Distinguished Service Medal for single-handedly wiping out 32 Viet Cong when his unit got caught in an ambush. "Us two are the most brutal," Guerrero asserted.

For the purposes of the book, I asked Chief Cochée if it would be possible to put Guerrero and Malachi together for one swing shift as a special wild-card patrol team. Actually, the idea was Guerrero's. "That way we won't have to answer routine calls, but will be free to go anywhere in the city," he reasoned. "And even if it's on the other side of the city, I'll get there first. We'll ask the chief to give us a good-running unit. We'll find you some action." Also along for the wild-card patrol was a photographer, who was hopeful that he would get some good pictures to illustrate this book.

With the guests sitting in the backseat, Guerrero tore out of the parking lot and careened around the first few corners. From riding with him before, I had learned that this was part of his procedure. He said he liked to get the feel of a particular car, and also test the brakes and rear end in some high-speed maneuvers. This time, though, Guerrero didn't stop his balls-to-the-wall driving after a few corners. With Malachi holding onto the shotgun and anything else that would support him, we swung hard around turns and "blew" red lights after Guerrero had checked quickly for oncoming traffic. The photographer had mentioned earlier that he would like to get some pictures from outside the car of Guerrero racing around a corner. Since this couldn't be done on a real Code 3 call, we decided it would have to be set up. Guerrero headed for the industrial section of town, where there would be virtually no traffic, and happily put the car through its paces while the photographer shot his pictures. After four or five high-speed, skidding turns, we headed back to town.

"Okay," said Malachi, who had sat quietly during the racing sequences, "let's go slow for a while. I'm tired of holding onto this seat."

Guerrero seemingly didn't hear his former partner. "I'm going to the garage and have them change the spark plug wires," he said.

"If you got 25 bucks you can buy a Tune Master," Malachi said mockingly.

"It goes like shit," complained Guerrero.

"It goes pretty good to me," said the photographer, who was holding on for dear life amidst his camera equipment.

At the garage, Guerrero complained to the mechanic: "It has no pickup and it craps out at 90."

A few minutes later, we were cruising in a residential neighborhood when Guerrero decided to "jack up" a couple of kids walking down the sidewalk. The cops had them lean against the hood of the patrol car and Malachi frisked them while Guerrero watched. As the photographer was busily snapping pictures from behind the kids (so their faces wouldn't show), other kids in the neighborhood began forming nearby in small groups. The spectators appeared more interested in the photographer's camera than in the cops.

"You guys want to get into the picture?" Malachi asked a group of them.

"Yeah! Yeah!"

"Okay," he said, taking his gun out. "Start running down the street." Malachi grinned as the kids quickly dispersed, suddenly disinterested in the camera.

Finding nothing on the two kids, the cops let them go. "Walk on the sidewalk and observe all laws," Malachi said to the departing youths.

To Guerrero, Malachi said: "I knew they couldn't

have done too much wrong. They didn't run."

Back in the car, the radio came alive with a 415 call. When the address came over the airwave, Guerrero accelerated and skidded around the first corner, headed for the action. Just as quickly, the radio informed everyone that the call was Code 4 [no further assistance required]. Guerrero slowed down.

"That was a nice corner," he observed.

"I wish you'd let us know what you are going to do," Malachi complained in a friendly tone.

At a stop sign, Guerrero pulled up behind an older car. Then, although there was only one lane for traffic going our direction, he squeezed the car around the right of the waiting car and stopped when the front bumpers were even. The young male driver, who was alone in the car, didn't turn his head. Guerrero leaned out the window slightly and craned his neck to check out inside the car. The driver was still frozen, and when traffic cleared he calmly proceeded across the intersection. Guerrero moved behind him and put on his red light. The driver immediately pulled over.

"There's no key in the ignition," Guerrero told Malachi as the latter picked up the radio mike.

"Yeah, the way he kept looking straight ahead wasn't normal, either," Malachi commented, more for the benefit of the backseaters.

The young black driver ended up having several outstanding tickets, no driver's license in his possession, and no current registration. (He had lost his ignition key, so he had punched the ignition in the same manner as auto thieves, consequently sparking Guerrero's suspicions.) But the two wild-card officers weren't in any report-writing mood this day. After Guerrero checked over the man's arms for needle marks, and found none, he let him go.

Officer Vic Guerrero checks a suspect's arm for needle marks; the man was driving without keys in the ignition.

But an earnest Malachi warned him. "If I didn't have my shit together, like you, I would get everything fixed so a policeman wouldn't even look at me."

Back on the road, Malachi talked about the last auto thief he had caught; an unfortunate fellow who was trying to steal Patrolman R. E. Allen's Porsche from the courthouse parking lot. "R. E. and I had to testify on this case, and we were coming out of the courthouse and R. E. says, 'Hey, there's a guy with a car just like mine.' I said, 'That is your car!' R. E. exploded, man. He took out his gun and yelled, 'Motherfucker, get out of my car!' Of course the guy got thumped in the parking lot. That's a rule if you get caught in a parking lot alone with me and R. E."

The wild-card car had a difficult time finding any action. It seemed like the action was always happening on the opposite side of town. We would start racing across town to a heavy call, but inevitably before we got there the call would be canceled. Despite Guerrero's best efforts, we were usually beat to the call by the district car that was much closer. Then, we would stay over on that side of town, and the next heavy call would come down on the other side. Vic was fit to be tied. Ron was tired of all the cross-town Code 3s.

"I don't enjoy myself with you," Malachi told Guerrero. "I think I'd rather be working by myself today, and not be in the book." Malachi looked at us in the backseat. "I used to ride with Vic the day before my days off. [All Compton patrolmen work four days on, three days off.] By the time the night was over, I was a nervous wreck. It took me my first two days off just to recuperate from his driving."

This time the 211 call was located several blocks away. At least we were on the right side of town. Guerrero ignited the afterburner and made it two blocks before the radio informed us that the owner of the liquor store had called the station to explain that he had hit the alarm by mistake.

"That doesn't mean anything," Guerrero explained, not slowing down. "We still have to roll to make sure someone doesn't have a gun to his head."

When we arrived, another patrol car was already in the parking lot. The two officers were inside the store.

Guerrero got out and walked toward the store with his hand on his holstered gun. Malachi unlatched the shotgun and approached the store with several yards between him and Guerrero. As he walked, Malachi whistled "Happy Days Are Here Again." The other two officers came out of the store smiling. It was a bona fide false alarm.

Guerrero and Malachi approach a liquor store on a robbery call. They keep a distance between them so as to make it difficult for one gunman to get them both.

"It's a false alarm," officers tell Malachi as he approaches a liquor store with a shotgun in hand. Robbery shootouts are frequent in Compton.

Back in the car, Guerrero put out a Ten-8 over the radio, then floored the gas pedal. Malachi grabbed for the shotgun barrel, and held on for the 57th time. "Man, I haven't figured out where you're going yet," said Malachi, "but we'll sure get there in record time."

"About time we go to the Red Garter," said Guerrero. "The swing shift is on."

"Every shift swings at the Garter," said Malachi.

For no apparent reason, Guerrero parked the patrol car on the wide sidewalk in front of the topless beer bar. The two cops leaned against their unit, each finishing cups of coffee that they had just picked up at Jerry's Drive-In, the favorite coffee shop and restaurant of the Compton patrol division. Several surprised customers exited the Red Garter and nearly bumped into the police car. A new Buick with a good-looking young woman driver pulled into the parking lot. She got out and approached the Garter.

"Hi, Candy," Malachi said.

"Hi, Ron. Vic."

She was carrying a small bikini bottom, and Vic playfully grabbed it from her and put it up to his nose. He sniffed audibly.

"Sorry, Vic," said Candy. "I just washed them."

Inside, the cops watched appreciatively as Candy went up on stage and did her routine to the music. Thirty minutes later it was time for the wild-card car to hit the streets again.

Cruising through a dark residential area, Guerrero stopped next to a car that was double-parked in the middle of the street. Two young black men were sitting in the front seat, and they both gave the cops a hard look.

"What are you doing?" Malachi asked the driver through his open window.

"Man, what's it to you?" the guy answered in his best punk tone.

"I'm going to ask you one more time," Malachi said with a controlled tone. "What are you doing?"

"What you going to do to me, pig? Beat me up."

Malachi looked over at Guerrero, who was enjoying the scene. Obviously, Vic was more than ready for a fight. Guerrero got out of the car, and Malachi followed. The passenger got out of the double-parked car and indicated he wanted no part of any fight scene. The driver stayed put, checking out the two big cops.

"Okay," said Malachi, waiting for the driver to make his move.

"Why you cops always have to harass people?" the driver said in a softer voice.

"Was I harassing you?" Malachi said. "You're sitting here blocking the street when there's plenty of parking at the curb, and I ask you a simple question and you come back with shit. We'll fight, if that's what you want to do."

Obviously the driver had changed his mind about a fight. He moved his car next to the curb, and Malachi and Guerrero got back into the patrol car. The passenger got back in the other car.

"Hey," Malachi told the driver, "every time I see you, you got a punk in the car. Aren't you interested in girls?"

"Aw, man," the embarrassed driver said.

"If you don't have a girl in the car next time I see you," Malachi continued, "I'm going to give you a ticket."

Guerrero drove on, and after several blocks of silence Malachi said solemnly, "His mouth is going to put him in the hospital. He's always talkin' bullshit."

In the same neighborhood, the patrol car passed a car parked in front of a house that had several young Mexicans standing around outside. Suddenly, a young man jumped out from behind the wheel of the car and walked up to the group. It was a suspicious move, as if he was trying to get away from something incriminating in the vehicle. Guerrero stopped and backed the unit up to the suddenly abandoned auto. The cops got out, and the group of youths watched closely as they flashed their lights in the car. Guerrero reached in and came out with an open can of beer. He put the half-filled can on top of the car, and opened the door for a more thorough search. Malachi motioned the young man who had exited the car to come over and stand next to him. He did. In the glove compartment, Guerrero found a small bottle of suspicious-looking pills. Meanwhile, Malachi had the driver open the trunk, where a long knife and large hatchet were covered by a rag. With all the paraphernalia spread out on the roof of the car, it looked like a sure bust. The driver knew it, and the young spectators knew it, but the cops fooled them all.

"Okay, put everything back in your car," Malachi told the surprised driver. "Look, man, cool it when it comes to drinking in the car. Okay?"

"Yeah, okay, I knew I shouldn't have," the driver explained. "And those pills, they're my mother's diet pills."

"Sure," Malachi said. "Pour them out on the street." The youngster did as he was told and Malachi stepped on them.

"Okay, you guys take it easy," Malachi said as he climbed back into the squad car. "There," he said to

Guerrero, "I did my good deed tonight for the Mexican community. Now let's go help some blacks. And some whites, too, if we can find any.'"

After another 30 minutes of cruising on the back streets, Guerrero brought the car back out on the main drag. Both he and Malachi were frustrated by the lack of any heavy action. "Why doesn't somebody rob something?" Malachi said disgustedly. "We'll tell some guy to rob something for the photographer and we'll have him coming out of the store with a gun for the pictures. Then we'll say 'we fooled you' and blow him up."

The beat sergeant put out a call on the radio for Guerrero and Malachi to call in on a street-box telephone. Guerrero stopped at a nearby police phone and called the station. "They asked us if we would start accepting radio calls now," he said. "I told them we would. What the hell, it's something to do."

The radio immediately ordered us to a 415 (family fight). "Here I thought we weren't going to work too hard tonight," Malachi observed wryly.

Malachi has a reputation within the department for his special ability to handle family fights. Often he can get the two combatants to end up laughing. One time a husband was complaining about his wife, and Malachi asked him to describe what she does to upset him. He related a long list of things and Malachi listened intently, then when the man stopped he said: "You know, my partner here has the same exact problems with his wife." Everyone cracked up.

But this case was different. A mother had been arguing with her 22-year-old son until the son exploded in a rage of fury and started busting up furniture. When

Malachi and Guerrero walked into the living room, it looked ransacked. The mother looked frightened and the son dangerous.

Malachi took the mother into the hallway to talk to her, and Guerrero stood silent watch over Larry, the son. Several minutes later Malachi came back with the mother and he sat down on an overturned cabinet across from the youth who was seated on the couch, the only piece of furniture in the room left upright.

"Larry, why didn't you leave the house when your mother asked you to?" Malachi asked.

"Look, this is my house, too. You dig!"

"It's your mother's house, Larry, and she asked you to leave because she didn't like the way you were acting. Why didn't you just take off for a while? Cool off?"

"Look, you try to take me from this house and you're going to have a fight on your hands," the youth warned.

Malachi returned the young man's intent stare. "Once I leave here tonight, if I have to come back, I will break your face," Malachi said evenly.

"Oh, you black traitor," the surprised kid sputtered. "Man, you're a pig. You're not a brother. I'm trying to go to school and I'm poor and don't have any money. You don't know nothing about the struggle."

"Don't tell me I don't know about the struggle," said Malachi. "I've been through it. I grew up in the ghetto. You and I both know you can do it without coming back and giving your mother a bad time. Why don't you just leave for a while?"

"Don't have any money," he said.

"I told him I'd give him a $200 check," the mother protested.

"He needs cash," Malachi said, suddenly on the son's side. "Don't you have any cash?"

"Think I got $5," she said.

"That's not enough," Malachi answered.

"Larry, isn't there anyone you can stay with for the night just until your mom's cashing a check tomorrow ?"

"No. Don't have any friends around here."

"I can go stay with someone," the mother volunteered. "Anything to get away from him."

"Okay, I think that's the solution for tonight," Malachi said, standing up. He watched as the mother gathered her purse and coat and went out the door. "Well, Larry, you got some thinking over to do. Listen, if you ever want to talk to me, you know, about school or anything, just call the station and ask for me. Now you stay cool and take care of yourself."

Larry nodded at Malachi. "Yeah. Thanks."

Back in the patrol car, Malachi said, "I hate for a guy to mouth off at his mother. He sure didn't like me telling him about busting his face. I'd like you to say that next time, Vic."

"I thought we had another one," said Guerrero. "Remember that guy who stood in the hallway with a stick and said we weren't going to come and get him?"

"Oh, yeah," said Malachi.

"I wanted to go get him," Guerrero explained. "Mommy didn't want me to. Ron [Malachi] wanted to drop to his knee and shoot six bullets in him."

"What else can you do when he's got a stick?" asked Malachi.

In 1970, a doctor found that Guerrero had an irregular heartbeat. It kept him out of the draft, but it also nearly eliminated him as an applicant for a policeman's job with the City of Compton. At the time, Guerrero wrote the following letter to the police department:

"If there is no other recourse for me to take, I will go get reclassified to 1-A and if necessary, I will not hesitate to enlist for two years, if this is a prelude that is required of me to reach my endeavor of a Law Enforcement career. I plan to exhaust every possible means open to me in a desperate attempt to get on your department. I'm willing to absorb any financial obligation of seeing a cardiologist (of the department's choice) if you deem it necessary in your consideration of me for candidacy."

A cardiologist subsequently submitted a report saying that Guerrero had an abnormally slow pulse rate, but that it was not harmful. The department kept him in contention for a patrolman's job.

An extensive background check was made, with 30 individuals and companies being contacted in regards to the character of one Victor Guerrero. A check with the Department of Motor Vehicles showed a driving tendency: seven moving violations, four within the last two years for tailgating and speeding.

Victor Guerrero was hired as a patrolman on July 1, 1971. An evaluation reported for the period July 1, 1972, to July 1, 1973, stated the following: "Officer Guerrero is performing very satisfactorily, he is outstanding in personal appearance and conducts himself as a trained and competent officer. He has been striving to improve himself in the area of community relations. Overall: competent."

The same evaluation found Guerrero "standard" on a long list of traits or performances, except for five "strong" ones and one "weak" one. The strongs were: neatness of work product, personal appearance, observance of work hours, application to duties, and performance in emergency. The weak area was: "meeting and handling the public."

The latter grade was given to Guerrero because of a number of incidents, one of which occurred in April, 1973, and resulted in his suspension without pay for two working days. The investigating officer's report stated the following: "Complainant alleges that he was arrested by Officers Guerrero and Jeffery at approximately 0255 hrs. on 19 April, 1973, at Centennial High School. And that Officer Guerrero kicked him in the stomach, pushed him against the wall, and kicked him in the groin area. Further that Officer Guerrero struck him three (3) times in jaw and in his right eye, causing lacerations which required that he receive medical treatment.

"This complaint, as it relates to the kicking of the subject in the stomach by Guerrero is sustained. With reference to the kicking in the groin area and causing injury to the subject's eye, there is no corroborating evidence to support this allegation and it is therefore not sustained.

"The question is whether Officer Guerrero's actions were warranted or not. An officer has a right and obligation to use only that force which is necessary to overcome force and/or resistance of the arrestee. . . . It is obvious that Officer Guerrero did not follow the proper 'pat down' procedure or he developed his own procedure which included kicking the suspect in the midsection, As a third point, Officer Guerrero is a trained and experienced karate practitioner and therefore should know how to prevent a suspect from coming off a wall during a search, that is, short of kicking the suspect in the midsection with his foot.

"Officer Guerrero alleges that the subject suddenly pushed himself from the wall and dropped his right arm out of this Officer's sight. Officer Guerrero then quickly moved back and kicked the subject in the stomach and then moved forward pushing the subject up against the wall.

"Officer Guerrero has had two (2) prior incidents in which there have been complaints from citizens alleging that he used excessive and unnecessary force in affecting arrest. Officer Guerrero has been advised and counseled by his supervisors regarding aforementioned situations.

"Based upon the information in this report it is my opinion that Officer Guerrero used excessive and unnecessary force by kicking the complainant in the stomach area with his foot."

This incident took place before Tom Cochée was hired as chief, and the acting chief, Captain Manuel Correa, sustained the investigating officer's report and wrote the following letter to Guerrero: "It has been determined that on 19 April, 1973, at approximately 0255 hrs. at Centennial High School, you kicked a 17-year-old male person in the stomach with your foot. Your actions in kicking the subject was an act of excessive and unnecessary force, considering the surrounding circumstances. It has been determined that your actions constitute misconduct and you are subject to disciplinary action. You are hereby notified that you are suspended without pay for two (2) working days—Friday, June 8, and Friday, June 15."

Guerrero shrugged off the incident. He said the investigating officer had a "hard on" for him and was out to nail him. Also, he claimed that the kid had a pair of scissors in his pocket when he came off the wall, and that his hand was disappearing in that direction. But whatever, Guerrero thinks the investigation was all too typical of a community relations-conscious police department that frowns on what he considers to be good police work. He said the cops who are lazy and stay in their cars and don't look for trouble never get personnel complaints against them. But the cops who work hard, often get out of their cars on investigations, make bar checks, and are otherwise active on the street always get complaints—usually unfair ones from people who are just upset at getting busted. It was these general frustrations that led Guerrero recently to ask to be transferred out of patrol. Chief Cochée quickly obliged him—for his own reasons—and Guerrero is now attached to research and planning.

Victor Guerrero then is a controversial cop. Named by many officers as the one they would want backing them up in a tough physical encounter, he is also viewed by some of his fellows as a strong-arm cop who likes to come down heavy on street people. As to why Chief Cochée didn't kick and scream at the thought of Guerrero wanting out of patrol, it was obviously a matter of public relations and law enforcement philosophy. Guerrero is not the kind of cop who will build up the department's public image. Although Guerrero may be good in fight situations and make a lot of good busts, Cochée apparently didn't feel the trade off was worth it.

• • •

A month before my "wild-card" ride with Guerrero and Malachi, I passed Guerrero in the police parking lot. Although I'd heard a lot about him, I had never met him.

"Say, you're Guerrero, aren't you?" I asked.

"Yeah, why?" Guerrero shot back, not even slowing down.

"I'm writing a book on this department and I've got to ride with you. I've heard a lot about you."

"I'm a dead-end street," he said in his machine gun-style delivery. "Going off patrol in two weeks. No more patrol."

"I'd still like to get with you," I said, trying to catch up to him.

"Okay. Go in and talk to the beat sergeant. You can go out with me today."

Sergeant Gary Taylor, a large black officer, said it would be all right for me to ride with Guerrero. (I always had in my possession a letter from Chief Cochée ordering his supervisory personnel to cooperate with me.) Taylor invited me to the swing shift briefing.

"All right, we have a 211-261 suspect [robbery-rape] from yesterday," said Taylor in an even voice. "He's a male Negro, 20 to 30, medium natural, wearing a brown leather jacket. . . ."

"Very good," one of the officers said mockingly.

"Okay, all you black officers are under arrest," said a white officer.

"All right, anyway, we've obviously got a burg-rape working the south eastside," Taylor continued. "So be on the lookout. . . ."

A few minutes later, Guerrero was climbing into his patrol car, complaining that he got stuck with a lemon.

"We're working the burglar-rapist area, but that description is totally useless," he explained. "Anyway, the guy's M.O. is morning, so I don't think we'll see him."

An hour after clearing the station, we got a strange radio call. Someone had telephoned the police station and said that Patty Hearst could be found in the vicinity of a downtown intersection. Although it was not a Code 3 call, Guerrero, who seemed uncharacteristically excited, drove at breakneck speeds and was the first policeman on the scene. He cruised up and down several nearby streets, going back and forth through the intersection. He asked one middle-aged man in the heavily Mexican-black neighborhood whether he had seen a young white woman with blonde hair. The perplexed man said no. Then, in a nearby alley, Guerrero spoke Spanish to several young Mexican girls standing on a back porch. They answered him, then, curious, wandered out to the patrol car. One of the girls continued the conversation in English.

"Who is it you're looking for?" she asked.

"Patty Hearst," Guerrero answered.

The girl laughed and said something to her friends in Spanish; they joined in the laughter. "Who wants that dumb girl?" she asked.

"The F.B.I. does," said Guerrero. "There's a reward, you know."

Guerrero drove the car out of the alley and pulled next to another patrol car. It was the beat sergeant, and he was taking a hard look at something across the street and down several hundred feet.

"No one's seen anything," Guerrero reported.

"Don't turn around, but there's some cottages down

there across the street," the sergeant said, as another patrol car pulled up and stopped abreast of the other two cars. "I saw a black guy and white woman in there, looking out several times from behind a curtain."

"Maybe we'd better have a look," Guerrero.

"Yeah, I think so," said the sergeant, picking up the radio mike to give orders to the six patrol cars that were now cruising within a five block area looking for the newspaper heiress. Within 60 seconds four patrol cars were cruising abreast down the street in one direction, and coming from the other way were two more units. They converged on the front cottage. One patrolman drove his car up on the grass in front of the residence and stopped about 15 feet from the front door. The door suddenly opened, and a big, husky black man stepped out, with a short, stocky, blonde white woman huddling protectively behind him.

"Hey, Jim, what's happening?" he said to one of the patrolmen.

"Harry, what the hell? . . ." the patrolman said.

The black man approached the officer and whispered something. The cop nodded his head, smiled, and walked to where the sergeant was standing.

"I know this guy, sarge," the patrolman said. "He's here cheating on his wife. That's all there is to it."

"Guess we don't get our names in the paper," another officer said.

Residents of the other cottages came out and asked what was going on. When they were told about the Patty Hearst report, everyone began cracking up. As the cop cars pulled away, the residents were still grouped around the front cottage, making jokes and laughing, some of them hysterically.

"I'd love to find Patty Hearst," Guerrero admitted as he drove out of the area to resume patrol. "I'd settle for anyone in the SLA. But Patty would be nice. If we did, it would really make your book a best seller, wouldn't it?"

•   •   •

That night a single shot rang out from gang-infested Park Village. The bullet missed the heads of patrolman John Wilkinson and his partner by inches, shattering the red light assembly atop their vehicle. Wilkinson immediately put out a "Code 9—Shots Fired at Officers" call, and every patrol car in the city raced to the scene.

Guerrero, who was in the station filling out a routine traffic accident report, dropped everything and ran to his car. Before he cleared the station lot, he put out on the radio: "ETA, 30 seconds." (ETA: estimated time of arrival). Although Park Village was nearly two miles away, if he missed the 30 seconds it wasn't by much.

Several patrol cars cruised Park Village, and when Wilkinson finally figured out the trajectory of the bullet, the cops searched several vacant buildings. The frustration of knowing there was a potential cop-killer here, but not being able to find him, began to show on their faces.

Patrolman Reuben Chavira, carrying his .357 down at his side, finally spat out: "Fuck the Chief's public relations. We ought to kill these bastards."

•   •   •

As the days neared when Guerrero would be reassigned to research and planning, he claimed to be looking forward to being out of patrol. He said he was tired of the poorly equipped police cars, the public relations bullshit, the punks in the street, etc., etc. He seemed to be trying to convince himself as well as others that he wouldn't miss patrol.

His last night on patrol, Guerrero told his partner, Patrolman Robert Quintana, that he wasn't going to get involved in anything. Quintana warned him that he had a bad attitude.

Midway through the watch, they received a 211 in-progress call at a nearby hamburger stand. As Quintana turned the car around and headed back in the direction of the call, Guerrero commented that the robbers probably would be gone by the time they got there.

"I told him, man, don't say that," Quintana recalled. "That's dangerous talk. When we got there, I stopped at the side of the place, and Vic jumped out and went around to the back door. I went to the front, and as soon as I got there I saw through the window that a guy had a sawed-off shotgun and was holding it on some hostages who were down on their knees. Just then . . . I couldn't believe it, but just then, the back door swung open, and Guerrero was standing right in the middle of the doorway, just like he expected to find nobody there. He didn't even have his gun drawn. The guy swung the barrel of the shotgun toward Guerrero, and it was pointed right at his stomach. Guerrero froze. There was nothing I could do, because if I shot I would either hit Guerrero or the hostages. For some reason the guy didn't fire, and Guerrero had time to swing the door closed. The guy gave up after we got more units there, but if he'd been high on drugs or desperate,

Guerrero would be a dead man today."

Typically, Guerrero shrugged off the incident. "I have very fast reflexes from karate. I could have jumped out of the way before the guy fired. When the other units got there, I yelled to Malachi, 'Bring the grenades.' The guy immediately gave up. Malachi and I both thumped on his head as we dragged him to the car."

For some reason, ex-Patrolman Victor Guerrero didn't learn his lesson that night. It seems he's still invincible.

CONCLUSION

Each time I left Compton after one of my visits, I had a nagging feeling for the next several days that I was missing something. And indeed I was.

A few days after one of my trips, the Compton National Guard armory was knocked off -- rifles, automatic weapons, machine guns, hand grenades -- enough armament to fully equip a combat-ready infantry company.

Shortly after that, a Compton cop was busted by the Compton narks for, well, you-can-imagine-what. That was soon followed by the accidental shooting of a bank guard by Patrolman Robert Quintana, the volatile Latin officer who took so much pride in his $55 bulletproof vest. Quintana, who had responded to a silent alarm at a bank, tells his side of what happened:

"I was a one-man unit and I got out of the car with my gun in my right hand. I peeked into the plate glass window and tapped my gun on the window. Nobody moved inside. Everyone was standing still. I figured it must have been a good alarm. I approached the front door, and when I got to the door I lowered myself to crouch position. It was unfortunate I did that because I lost my balance and hit the ground with my right shoulder. My gun fired and a bullet struck the security guard in the leg." (There were no bank robbers inside. When the alarm went off accidentally, the elderly guard told everyone in the bank to stand still.)

A local, ambulance-chasing TV station played up the accidental shooting as an assassination attempt, and the public heat increased when it was discovered that Quintana was under investigation by the sheriff's department for alleged shooting into a neighbor's home. He was cleared of that incident when he proved he was in Compton with two other off-duty policemen at the time it happened.

Concerning the accidental shooting at the bank, Chief Cochée indicated to me that Quintana was carrying a "defective weapon," and also that the officer refused to take a lie detector test. For these reasons, Cochée fired him.

"My gun was checked out in the lab and found to be in good condition," Quintana claims. "The tip of my hammer was broken off, but you don't pull the hammer back to fire the gun anyway. You pull the trigger. No, the chief didn't fire me for the gun. He fired me for refusing to take a polygraph."

Quintana asserts that the chief did not give him a direct order to take the test -- otherwise, he would have taken it, knowing full-well that he faced immediate dismissal if he refused a direct order. But regardless of the exact circumstances and technicalities, Quintana lost his job.

If at this point anyone is expecting some crisp, conclusive judgments from me regarding what is portrayed in this book, I'm going to disappoint. I'm still undecided about much of it myself. What I have tried to do in these pages is give an honest account of what I saw and heard firsthand.

I hope I have been fair to the city, the chief, and his officers. It will be up to you, the reader, to draw your own conclusions about what you've read, and decide whether you like the job the first black police chief in California is doing and whether you like the caliber and personalities of the policemen I rode with. In every situation, I let them speak for themselves.

• • •

Police Chief Tom Cochée: "Why did I open up the department to author Bruce Henderson? Well, for better or worse, that's my style. I believe in openness and laying things out on the table for everyone to see. Naturally, I hope there is a beneficial and positive aspect to the book project, but I'm surely not making that a requirement for my cooperation. Sitting in the patrol car next to the police officer and observing him in action is really the only way to truly understand the job of fighting crime, as well as the horrendous pressures on the police profession in this day and age."

Made in the USA
Charleston, SC
23 November 2014